A Curse of Flames and Magic

Jade Lafontaine

Jade Lafontaine/Cristelli Publishing
Montreal, QC, CANADA
http://cristellipublishing.wordpress.com

Author's Note: This is a work of fiction. Names, characters, places, and incidents are a product of the author's imagination. Locales and public names are sometimes used for atmospheric purposes. Any resemblance to actual people, living or dead, or businesses, companies, events, institutions, or locales is entirely coincidental.

A Curse of Flames and Magic/ Jade Lafontaine. -- 1st ed.
ISBN 9798360241218

Dedicated to one of my best friends, Melinda Moffitt.

A real friend is one who walks when the rest of the world walks out.

–WALTER WINCHELL

Table of Contents

Chapter One

I was not what you would consider normal. I was not even average by the standards of those who were different. If you're asking yourself why I was not ordinary, I will gladly tell you. I was not considered normal by regular people and supernatural creatures because I was a halfbreed. I was a rarely-created hybrid that was born every one thousand years.

I was a hybrid that was also not accepted at all once born. The type of halfbreed that I am is a demon and a witch. My species was a rarity because demons and witches did not mate. It was uncommon that you'd ever find a demon and a witch as mates and very unlikely that you'd see their children too.

The reason demons and witches rarely mated was that demons lacked boundaries when dealing with witches. Demons were creatures that loved to spread chaos, especially toward witches. They also loved to feed off the chaos, hatred, and war as if they were bloodthirsty vampires.

Demons were horrible creatures that would cause death and destruction rather than leave the world peaceful. Because of this, demons loved to cause mayhem within the magic community, especially among witches, due to our sisterly bonds. They loved to break those bonds and watch us practically tear each other apart.

My mother, a commonly known and all-powerful witch within our people, was also the Supreme, the highest ranking leader because the title has been passed from generation to within our family. She was all I had in this world, my father and my mentor.

My mother was a gorgeous woman. She had high cheekbones, beautiful bronze skin, well-rounded lips, a curvy yet petite body, amber-hued eyes, shoulder-length black hair that used to be down to her back, and a frame that stood at the height of 5'9. My mother was also the type of woman who didn't take shit from anyone whatsoever. She was a just and fair ruler within our community, and she did not abuse her power at all, nor did she use her ability to take advantage of others' weaknesses or strengths.

My mother was the most excellent supreme of her time. Another thing was that my mother was one of the witches throughout the time that would give birth to the child of a demon every black moon.

I say black because the moon turned black every thousand years when a witch and a demon mated. It just so happened on the night I was one that, the moon had turned entirely black in the sky. This alarmed many humans and supernatural creatures alike, especially humans because the moon that was once a bright off-white color was now a glowing black color. It wasn't that there was a solar eclipse that night, but it was just that a demon child was being born.

Because I was a rare hybrid, many supernatural creatures, especially vampires, tried to come after me. They all failed because both ends of the witch and demon spectrum protected me.

Most beings desired me so I could bring chaos and destruction, while others wanted me dead because I was a disgrace to the supernatural people. This was because mating with demons was the most frowned upon for all creatures. So if a devil and any other creature mated, they would be killed by others. It was a horrible thing, but it was a sad reality. When my mother discovered that destiny fated her to my father, she hid from everyone in the coven.

My mother avoided my father for hundreds of years until he had finally cornered her and had her submit to him. Once she was pregnant with me, she no longer hid her bond to my father from the coven. My mother, having expected disgusted reactions, was surprised when the coven embraced her with open arms.

The coven did not mind that my mother mated a demon, nor did my grandmother. They still loved her no matter what. I can say that all of the witches loved her because my aunt, my mother's sister, hated demons with a passion. My aunt had tried to kill my mother and me simultaneously with a few other witches. My aunt's evil plans had come to light within the community, and she was murdered horribly by my father.

As for my father, he wasn't just any old demon. He was the demon king of Nazareth. My father was over three thousand years old, yet he still looked like he was in his early thirties. My father had short curly black hair that he usually kept short, copper skin with red undertones to it, well-curved lips, piercing black eyes, a toned and lean body, and two pairs of canines on each side of his mouth on both his top and bottom row of teeth.

My father, like most demons, fed off of chaos, hatred, and war, but his feeding upon these three things was very great due to his immense thirst for it. His appetite for it was so great that he would sometimes create wars throughout history just for the hell of it, no pun intended.

As the king of Nazareth, my father could also sense the very things he craved. Anywhere in the world that all those things popped up, he would know about it, then he would show up wherever it was and feed off it.

Despite my parents' significant titles within the supernatural world, they always made time for each other no matter what. My parents have been in love for centuries and will continue to be that way until time. As for their parenting skills, they were excellent parents who loved and cared for me. They still do, to be honest, and it's pretty overbearing sometimes, but I love them all the same.

When I turned thirteen years old, I came into my powers as a demon. My father was too busy ruling Nazareth to teach me how to control them, so he had his trusted mentor, Alan, teach me how to manage them. Alan was a great teacher, a bit of a hard-ass, but a great teacher nonetheless.

When I turned sixteen, my powers as a witch appeared. Since my mother, like my father, was busy, she had her mentor, Nyra, teach me how to control my powers. You'd think it's overwhelming to learn how to handle two different powers simultaneously, but I'll tell you it's not. It was effortless because I had a better grasp of control over my demonic forces than anything since I was a fast learner.

My powers, my demonic and magical powers, in a way, boosted each other to their full potential. My demonic abilities enhanced my magic powers, and my magical powers increased my demonic skills. They balanced each other out in a way that made me sort of a threat to all creatures alike. My parents were proud that I could control both powers without hurting myself, and they were both also proud again for two different reasons.

My mother was firstly proud because she wanted me to become the next supreme within our coven; the second was that I wouldn't hurt myself. The first reason my dad was proud was that he wanted me to take the throne in Nazareth as the demon queen and also because I could use my demonic powers without hurting myself again. Because of these reasons, my parents have been in this same argument for eight years. It's a never-ending argument that a simple kiss-and-make-up won't solve.

I've tried to find a standard solution for this, like telling them that maybe I can be the supreme and the demon queen, but they both said to me that I had to pick one or the other, then proceeded to ground me for two years for that 'foolish suggestion.' Honestly, I don't know if I'm ready to be the ruler of demons or a coven. It seems overwhelming and stressful because I have to worry about upholding the same legacy as my parents, two great rulers within their communities.

Chapter Two

The feeling of leaves, sticks, and pine cones stung the bottoms of my feet as I ran through the forest. My feet were covered in dirt and cut to my calf, my hair had leaves and sticks embedded into it, and my arms, my precious arms, were pitch black, along with my hands that had elongated sharp nails. Dark red lines were on my arms and hands like veins. My teeth had canines on each row like an ordinary demon's teeth, and my eyes were pitch black, including the whites.

I ran as fast as I could through the woods until something threw me back into a tree. My back hit the tree, and pain shot up my back. I fell four feet down to the ground onto the hard forest floor. The tree groaned from the force of having a powerful, blunt object hit it. The tree snapped and started to fall. I used my demonic powers to sink into the ground. I used my powers to teleport me far away from the tree.

"Goddamn it, Eve," I hissed, "Couldn't you have gone a little easier on me?"

"There is no such thing as going 'easier' on someone when you're in battle," Alan rolled his eyes as he appeared from the shadows,

"As much as I would hate to agree with this man, Alan's right, kid," Nyra stated as she appeared from a flurry of leaves.

"Your enemies will never go easy on you, Amora. You need to get that through your thick skull," Alan scolded, "Your enemies will do any and everything they can to hurt you, no matter what. When they notice you slowing down, your enemies will use your weakness against you and hurt you or, worse, kill you. This is why your friend here uses all her strength to hurt you. She's preparing you for the worst-case scenario, although she isn't as strong as her family name suggested."

"I resent that, you bastard," Eve growled inhumanely.

"Growl at me all you like, dog," Alan spat, "But know that I am telling the truth. You are much weaker than your brethren, especially your uncle and father."

"That man only knows how to do two things," Nyra remarked as she came up beside me, "Piss people off and create chaos."

"You're telling me," I muttered.

"I am not weak!" Eve snapped. Alan said nothing else and shot a black liquid at Eve. She didn't move in time, and the liquid speared her through her bicep. Eve cried out in pain and fell to one knee. She grasped the liquid, which had now hardened, and pulled it out as she grit her teeth. She threw it on the ground and glared at Alan as her wound closed.

"You bastard!" she growled.

"We might want to stop them before somebody gets killed," Nyra remarked. The sound of bones crackling and growling soon reached our ears. I knew then that Eve had transformed into her wolf form. Eve soon started to charge at Alan. I ran over toward those two. Just as Eve was getting ready to go for Alan's throat with her teeth and just as Alan was getting ready to raise his arm, I moved in the middle of them both, and I pushed Alan's arm up, then I made sure to move my other arm up as well. Eve sank her teeth into my arm and practically ripped it clean from its socket. I screamed in pain like a wounded animal. Alan shot a blast I knew would've instantly killed Eve into the sky, causing all birds and creatures to flee quickly from the trees. Eve jumped back at the realization of what she had done. Eve transformed back to her human form. Since her clothes had ripped from her transformation, she stood naked before us.

"Amora, I'm....I'm.....I'm....oh my god," She fell to her knees, and soon she started to cry. I moved away from Alan, and then I solidified my blood. I could coagulate my blood since I was half demon. It came in handy when I was training like this with Alan and Nyra. Not only has my arm been ripped off my body, but so have my hands or legs over the years. The shit that hurt the most was my fingers because, as a witch, I needed my hands to perform rituals and use spells, and as a demon, I needed my hands to bring down chaos upon the world. I was pretty used to this shit, but that didn't mean it didn't hurt like a bitch. I picked up my hand and walked over to Eve. I stared at her for a moment before slapping the shit out of her with my dismembered arm. Her head snapped sideways from the impact of the slap.

"Shut the hell up, you emotional idiot!" I hissed.

"What the hell did you hit me for?" she yelped.

"Because you're sitting here crying as if you murdered me or something," I snapped.

"I ripped your arm off your body! Don't you think that would make anybody feel bad?!" she yelled.

"Did you forget I'm a half-witch and half-demon, stupid?! I can solidify my blood and reattach it!" I growled.

"Well, I forgot! Sue me!" she growled back.

"If I could sue you, I would sue you for being a dumbass!" I bellowed.

"Oh, ha ha! Where'd you get that comeback? Lame-comebacks-for-idiots-dot-com?" she shot back. Eve transformed again, and I prepared for what was coming. Nyra suddenly appeared between us.

"Girls, that's enough for now. How about we call it a day, hm?" Nyra suggested.

"We've been out here for twelve hours, witch," Alan spat, "Amora needs all the training she can get. She's still far too weak."

"Then I guess you'd like to report to Valrick why his precious daughter passed out from exhaustion?" Nyra smirked.

"Fine," Alan venomously spat again. "She can rest, but she has to be here at this same spot at the crack of dawn. Tomorrow's training will run into the next day."

"Well, girls. Let's head back to my place for some tea and some of my famous Toad soup," Nyra announced.

"Awesome!" Eve cheered.

"And let's see if I can do something about the scarring that's going to appear after we reattach this arm," Nyra scolded. She took my arm from me, and suddenly it floated in the air. Nyra wrapped my limb in a cloth with silk ribbons on it.

"There we go," Nyra smiled, "Much better than looking at a severed arm, I tell you."

"Amora, the crack of dawn. No later than that," Alan gravely warned me.

"Yes, sir," I groaned. Alan soon turned into a shadow on the forest floor and quickly darted out of sight.

"Ready?" Nyra asked.

"Yes," Eve and I responded in unison.

Chapter Three

Nyra transported the three of us to another forest. Unlike the one we were in before, this forest burst with many more trees that looked dark everywhere.

"You girls know what to do, right?" Nyra asked. Eve and I both nodded.

"Good. Make sure you don't fall behind, girls," Nyra sang. An old black, wooden broom with a crooked handle and a black tail adorned with a white feather suddenly appeared through the trees. Nyra tied the lantern to the end of her broom and sat on it sideways. Eve soon transformed into her beautiful dark brown wolf that had some light brown here and there. I soon began to take on a more demonic form.

My canines started forming, and the nails on my remaining arm elongated. My eyes turned pitch black, and I felt my horns begin to come through as well. My horns will poke through when I take on half of my demonic or full-on demonic form. Right now, I'm taking on my total devilish shape, which causes my horns to come out fully.

My horns are pitch black, form at the top of my forehead, and curve backward. Sometimes if I take on my full demonic form, my horns will stay for months at a time. It's a pain to walk around with horns in the real world, considering how humans will either look at me weirdly or ask me how I got them to look like this or what kind of prosthetics I use. It gets very annoying, and I curse my father for making me like this, although I can't put a curse on him for real because he'll deflect it.

I remember in elementary school, and yes, I did go to elementary school like normal humans do, when my mother always had to look up different hairstyles for me to wear to school so my horns wouldn't show. I couldn't even participate in recess or gym class because of it. It wasn't until I hit middle school and started training to control the demonic powers that I could finally hide them. It wasn't easy, but I managed to do it. Even though I have control of my demonic forces, it's always tricky to get rid of my horns.

"Ready, girls?" Nyra asked. Eve and I nodded.

"Let's go!" Nyra jetted off on her broom. Eve ran after, and I turned into a shadow on the forest floor. I darted through the dangerously uninviting forest that I've known like the back of my hand since childhood.

We had finally reached Nyra's home, an old cottage buried deep within these woods surrounded by trees. Nyra's place looked like something out of some Disney movie; the aged wood varied from a light to a dark gray with a matching roof. Vines curled around the house's columns like snakes supporting the rooftop. There was a small porch on the front where an old rocking chair sat on the left of the old wooden door and a small basket on the right side of the door, usually used for picking herbs in these woods. At the top of the house was a chimney made from cobblestones.

"Home sweet Home," Nyra smiled softly as she hopped off her broom. She untied the lantern from her broom and took the broom into her hand. She walked over to the house and placed the lantern onto a thick, black metal stand curved over and down. We all walked inside the house together, and instantly the lights came on. Nyra placed her broom next to the door.

"Amora, light a fire for us, will ya?" Nyra asked.

"Sure," I nodded. I raised my index finger, and a flame danced on the tips of it. I aimed my finger at the fireplace, and the little fire shot directly toward the wood. Soon, the fireplace lit up completely.

"Thank you," She nodded.

"Nyra, any chance that you have some clothes for me?" Eve asked.

"Go look in Amora's room, and there should be a pair of sweatpants and a tank top for you," She informed the young wolf.

"Cool. Thanks, Nyra," Eve smiled.

"You're welcome, kid," Nyra smiled, "Amora, Come sit so I can reattach that arm of yours." I walked over toward Nyra as Eve disappeared down the hallway and sat down.

"Alright, kid. You know what to do," Nyra prompted. I stopped solidifying my blood as Nyra took my arm, and I wrapped it. A needle and a small roll of red thread appeared next to her. Nyra placed my detached arm at the base of where Eve tore it off. The stitching started, sewing my arm back together. I could feel myself beginning to heal as the thread fluidly stitched my arm. I winced as the needle poked through my skin.

Once that was over, Nyra caught the needle and thread as soon as it was about to drop. She walked away from me and towards the table where a small black box was. She unlocked it and then placed them inside gently. She closed the box and locked it. She walked towards an old black cabinet on the wall next to the fireplace, opened it, and started looking through it.

"That's old," She threw a jar behind her, and a trash can floated behind her and caught it. She continued to throw some things out until she found what she was looking for.

"Aha! Found it," She exclaimed. She walked towards me with a medium-sized jar filled with a dark green paste-like substance. She opened the pot, and a very putrid smell made its way out of the jar and into my nose. The smell started to burn my nostrils due to my heightened sense from my demonic side of the family. Nyra dipped her hand into the jar and walked towards me. She rubbed the dark green paste around my arm where the tissue had scarred after healing.

"We'll just leave this on for a few minutes seconds, and then you can take a shower," Nyra informed me.

"Okay," I nodded. Moments later, Eve walked into the room wearing a black tank top, a pair of gray sweats, and a pair of black socks.

"Nyra, do you mind giving me some shoes?" Eve asked.

"Sure," Nyra pointed her finger at Eve's feet, and a pair of slippers appeared on them.

"Thanks," Eve smiled.

"You're welcome," Nyra replied.

"Amora, your teeth haven't returned to normal," Eve asked.

"What?" I reached up and touched my teeth. I groaned loudly. She was right. My teeth, like my horns, hadn't become normal again.

"I sometimes wish my dad wasn't a demon. It's a hassle having these damn horns and teeth," I grumbled.

"Did somebody say, dad?" I heard from the door.

"Hello, Mr. V," Eve greeted.

"It's a pleasure as always to see you, Eve," My dad smiled at her. Unlike the rest of his subjects, who detested wolves, my dad liked Eve, even though she was a wolf. He liked her because she stuck with me for years as my best friend. He also tolerated her because she was very loyal to me and would protect me with her life as I would do her. My dad pretty much treated Eve like his second child, and Eve treated my dad like her second father.

"I guess you and Alan almost got into a scuffle?" He looked over at me.

"Yeah, we did," She looked down guiltily.

"No matter. It's quite alright, Eve, but you shouldn't let your anger get the best of you when dealing with someone like Alan. It would help if you remembered that he's thousands of years older than the three of us combined in this room. He does not have the patience for younger girls such as you and Amora, which means he will not hesitate to kill those that agitate him," My dad explained, "But remember that if you let your anger get the best of you. You end up harmed in any way when it comes to Alan, then think of how Amora would feel. She'd be inconsolable if something happened to you."

"Yes, sir," Eve nodded. Eve sat down at the table.

"As for you, my precious little demon, try not to get your limbs torn off so much. It's a little tedious to you and Nyra to reattach the same limbs repeatedly," my dad scolded.

"I'm alright, Alan. It gives me enough chances to perfect this little formula of mine that prevents scarring," she assured him.

"I know that, but it'll get tiring to reattach the same limbs repeatedly. She has to remember that when it comes to battling powerful enemies that she won't just sacrifice an arm or two, she's going to sacrifice her entire body as well," My father explained.

"Dad, please," I sighed.

"I'm telling the truth, Amora. You can't just go around losing limbs like it's nothing. You must ensure you don't lose so many at a time. Your enemies can use your loss of limbs against you," He added.

"I understand that dad, but right now, I need you two to help me with two of my biggest enemies," I told him.

"And what might that be?" He asked.

"Do you not see this, dad?" I questioned, gesturing to my teeth and horns.

"I do, and I don't see what the problem is," He replied.

"Dad, the problem is that I can't walk around humans with these things out. They'll start asking questions and trying to touch me as if I'm some science project," I murmured.

"I don't see why you're ashamed of the two aspects that are apart of your demonic heritage," He sighed.

"I'm not ashamed of them, dad, but it's just that when I go into the city, I have to encounter humans. It's a little annoying having them looking at me strangely, asking questions, and touching me," I cringed.

"Fine," he rolled his eyes. He touched my horns, and they sunk back into my head.

"I'm done," he sighed.

"What about the teeth, dad?" I asked. He groaned loudly and touched the side of my cheek lightly. My teeth turned back to normal.

"Thanks," I smiled.

"Yeah, yeah. Now has your mother been?" he inquired.

"Dad?" I sighed in exasperation.

"I'm just asking a question. A man can't ask a question?" He replied.

"You can, but you can also get the answer to that same question yourself by asking my mother, your mate, how she's been doing," I answered.

"You know I can't do that, Amora," he warned.

"Why? Because you two are fighting over me being the next supreme or demon queen?" I inquired.

"Exactly," he nodded. I groaned while Nyra and Eve laughed.

"Plus, your mother is probably worried about me anyway," he guessed.

"I would think so, considering how you two are mates," I replied in a 'duh' tone.

"Just tell me what I want to know before I force those sharp teeth of yours to come back out along with the horns," he muttered.

"You wouldn't dare," I gasped.

"Try me," he smirked.

"That's evil, dad," I gasped.

"I was born evil, Lani. Now tell me what I want to know," He responded.

"Fine. Mom is in Europe, and she's meeting with some witches that have some problems with the vampires in that area," I informed.

"What part of Europe?" He asked. As soon as I was about to tell him, my voice suddenly went out. I groaned deeply at the realization of what it was.

"Damn it. Did she put a spell over you that prevents you from telling me her location?" He fumed. I nodded.

"That damn woman is just as infuriating as the day I met her. You know she blocked me from her mind?" He ranted, "Who the hell blacks their mate from their mind? Who?!"

"My mother is who," I grumbled.

"I can't wait to see that woman so I can give her a piece of my fucking mind," My dad seethed. Nyra and Eve laughed again.

"Nyra, your former student is as stubborn as a mule," my dad seethed.

"Don't come complaining to me about it, Valrick. Talk to her when she gets back," Nyra replied with a small smile.

"And when will that be?" he asked.

"Well, she will come back in two days. You can talk to her then and talk about your grievances," Nyra informed.

"Oh. I will," He firmly stated. My dad kissed me on the forehead. I soon felt my horns starting to come out.

"What the hell, Dad?! We had a deal," I cried out.

"Since you allowed yourself to have a spell placed upon you, your horns are here to stay until you learn how to retract them on your own," He smirked at me.

"I didn't allow her to do anything. She probably did it when I wasn't paying attention," I rebuffed.

"Oh, you admit it was your fault that you allowed her to place a spell upon you?" He asked.

"I dislike you," I mumbled in irritation.

"I love you too, Amora," He smiled.

"Love you too," I grumbled.

"Eve, it was a pleasure seeing you as always," my dad smiled.

"You too, Mr. V," Eve smiled.

"Nyra, thank you for having me and for looking after my little girl," my dad grinned.

"A demon with manners, that's new," Nyra joked.

"Well, I can't be rude and disrespectful towards the woman who helped me and my beautiful mate raise this fine young woman sitting here today," he smiled.

"A charmer as always like your father," Nyra beamed.

"Well, I must say that it runs in the family," my dad mused.

"I'm sure it does," Nyra smiled again.

"Well, I must go before my advisors start sending out a search party for me," he chuckled as he buttoned one of the buttons on his blazer. I got up and hugged my father, and he hugged me back and kissed my forehead.

"I'll see you again soon, my precious child," he cooed.

"You too, Dad," I replied. We pulled away from each other, and he turned into a shadow on the floor. My dad walked over to the fireplace and stepped in. Soon the flames turned a brilliant blue, and they engulfed him.

"Alright, girls. Let's get started on dinner," Nyra announced.

4

Chapter Four

"Amora, breakfast is ready!" Nyra called from the kitchen. I yawned as I sat up in my bed. I scratched my shoulder and looked around my room. My room was a medium-sized space with a small window under my bed and a queen-sized black brass bed. I had a black nightstand on one side of my bed with a black lamp that had a white shade over it. My black dresser was against the wall near my door with a mirror above it.

On the right side of my room was a small black bookshelf filled with many spell books that identified different types of plants, roots, curses, cures, and potions.

On top of that, there was a large glass dome with a small pedestal with a cursed orchid inside. On the other side was my closet, with many clothes and shoes. I had a light inside of the closet, so I had to struggle with finding what I wanted to wear. Last but not least, I had an old black trunk my mother gave me that had a blanket of mine folded on top of it.

Inside the trunk were some things my dad gave me, such as a cursed musical box, a family heirloom passed down through his family for generations, and the skulls of a two-headed snake my dad had killed in Nazareth. I didn't know why he thought the heads of a two-headed snake would be an excellent gift for his daughter, but I kept it anyway because it's the thought that counts.

A light tapping on my window causes me to look over and see my familiar sleek black feline companion in the window. I stretched for a bit before turning around and opening the window. The black cat I've known since birth jumped through the window gracefully and landed on my bed. I flicked my wrist, and the window closed gently.

Salem, a two-thousand-year-old human trapped inside a cat's body, was a close companion of mine. Salem has been around my family since before the Salem Witch Trials and before Salem was an actual town. Salem has been loyal and helped my family for a thousand years since her entrapment inside that body. Salem was a trustworthy creature that not only looked out for us but gave great advice when a problem stumped us.

"Where have you been all night?" I asked.

"If you must know, I was out attending to things that your mother asked me to do," She replied.

"Like what?" I asked.

"The Fae are having problems with troublesome human children who are trespassing on their land and destroying everything on it," She explained.

"Damn humans," I muttered under my breath.

"The King of the Fae said the same thing after he explained the situation to me. He's more upset that they're trespassing onto their land when there's a sign outside of the forest warning them that they're not allowed even to set one foot inside," She informed me.

"So what did you do?" I asked.

"I set up a strong barrier around the forest that causes the humans to hallucinate and see terrible things when they walk through. The barrier will not affect us, otherworldly creatures, for we know our boundaries regarding each other's kingdoms," She responded.

"Can you tell me anything else?" I asked.

"Yes. The King requests the presence of you and your mother in terms of you marrying his eldest son," She replied. I groaned loudly. One thing I immensely detested about being the daughter of two powerful beings is that many royal nobles would request the presence of either my mother and me or my father and me to discuss marriage to their eldest sons. It got on my nerves so much to even have them do that.

I understood they wanted their sons to have a powerful being by their side, but honestly, it was too much. It's almost impossible for me to even have a mate in the first place since I am the first half-demon and half-witch child in a thousand years. Me finding a mate was a one-in-a-million chance. Even if I did find a mate, I wouldn't be able to take over as Supreme or Demon Queen. I'd have to devote my life to being by my mate's side 24/7, and who wants that? Not me.

"You can't blame these royals in our supernatural world for wanting you to marry their sons. They know the legend of a half-witch half-demon that's more powerful than any other creature combined. They know that finding a mate is nearly impossible too because you're so rare, but think of what you'd gain from it," Salem explained.

"Gain what? A third responsibility I have to think of is? If I become ruler of whatever kingdom I choose, I'll have to choose whether I'll be the Supreme or the Demon Queen. I don't want to worry about that," I cringed.

"Until you find a mate, you can't do much about it. You'll either have to marry into a noble family and bear the eldest son's children or find your mate, which is almost impossible," she told me.

"I know," I sighed, "It's just that I don't want to marry into those royal families. They're horrible people, especially to my father and my mother. Who knows how they would treat me."

"I understand your concern for your parents, but I assure you that they can handle the snide remarks of nobles," she remarked. "I can also assure you that those nobles won't lay a finger on you either. Why? Because your parents, as soon as they detect the slightest hint of abuse, will bring chaos upon those horrid creatures, especially your father." I smiled at the thought of what she said. Salem was right. My parents would bring hell upon earth if they saw someone trying to harm me.

That's just how they were, especially my father. I remember one time when I was six, I was at school, and this little human shit named Davy Matthews pushed me down on the playground and tried to force me to show him my horns after he had seen them one day when I thought nobody was looking. Our teacher, who was friends with Davy's mother, ignored Davy and his friends' horrible antics.

My father, who was with my mother the entire time watching them bully me, suddenly appeared at the school door with my mother, who tried to convince him to calm down. My father went to the playground and walked over to Davy and his friends. He used a glamour on the teachers and other humans that might've been passing by so that they didn't see his terrifying demonic form, but he showed Davy and his shithead friends, causing them to piss and shit their pants entirely.

He threatened to take their and their parents' souls if they ever treated me like that again. He made sure to haunt their dreams for three months so that they would get the message and they got the news. After that incident, they left me alone for the rest of our elementary days. My parents were terrifying creatures who'd kill all creatures if they dared to lay a finger on me.

"Now quit your complaining and go wash up for breakfast. Nyra has gone all out again for your benefit," Salem murmured.

"She always goes to such great lengths to keep me happy," I murmured.

"Can you blame her? She loves you as if you were her child," Salem informed me. I smiled softly.

"I know," I responded.

"Well, now that you know, let's go eat," she stated. I nodded. I got out of my bed and slipped on my house shoes. Salem jumped to the floor with unmatched grace. I walked behind her towards my door, which swung open. We walked into the large kitchen together. I sat down at the kitchen table. Nyra walked over and sat a plate of pancakes with bacon and eggs in front of me.

"Thank you, Nyra," I smiled.

"You're welcome," She smiled back. I started to dig into my food while Nyra danced and sang around the kitchen to Stevie Nicks.

"Alan canceled today's training session, so how about you join me when I visit the Black Fang pack?" She suggested.

"Sure. Why are you visiting Eve's pack?" I questioned.

"The former alpha king sent a messenger earlier this morning telling me that they needed help with an urgent matter," She replied, "I thought it best that I bring you along so you can get a little more experience."

"Sure. Anything to see Eve today," I replied.

"Then it's settled," she agreed, "Finish up your breakfast and get dressed." I nodded.

After breakfast, I helped clean up the kitchen using magic until Nyra scolded me and said I shouldn't use it for such small things. I cleaned the kitchen normally before going to get dressed.

Once I was done with my shower, I dried off using my magic then I moisturized my body with Palmer's and Vaseline. I got dressed in a black body con dress with spaghetti straps, a pair of black peep toe lace-up heels with a chunky block heel, and a black leather jacket. I put my curly hair into two top knots with some hanging down. I looked in the mirror and sighed because my horns were still out. It's been two days since my dad practically forced me to wear my horns out.

"Amora, you ready?" Nyra called me.

"Yeah, I am," I replied. I walked out of my room and into the kitchen.

"What's going to be our mode of transportation?" I asked.

"Fire," She replied.

"Why fire?" I questioned.

"It's easier than riding a broom or teleporting

"That's true," I agreed.

"Mhm. Now let's go," she pressed. We both stepped into the fireplace and engulfed a brilliant blue flame. Instead of feeling a horrible burning sensation, I felt a very comfortable, warm feeling around my body that made me feel warm on the inside. Pretty soon, we teleported outside of the Black Fang pack's main house. Soon we were approached by two pack members, a tall, dark-skinned man with skin that looked as smooth as silk and a man with olive skin that was almost as beautiful as his counterparts.

"Hello, gentlemen," Nyra greeted, "I'm here to speak with your former alpha, Bastian." The tall, dark-skinned pack member growled when he saw me.

"What is that demon bitch doing with you?" He spat. He might be attractive on the outside but horrid on the inside.

"Demon bitch?" I snapped, feeling irritated. The man growled at me along with his partner. I could feel my nails growing longer as my hands and part of my arm turned black with red veins. My teeth become sharp like a dog on the top and bottom row. My horns grew a little more in size, and my eyes turned pitch black. My tongue soon began to grow as well.

"I'll make you regret those words, dog," I spat venomously. The two wolves started to transform, but they stopped at the sound of a firm, deep voice. Both wolves returned to normal, and they looked behind at a man who didn't look a day over fifty walking towards us.

"Caius, Armand. Why didn't you tell me that my guest had arrived?" The man asked in irritation.

"Sir, the witch has a demon with her," The dark-skinned man informed. The man looked over at Nyra and me.

"Nyra, why did you bring a demon with you?" The man asked angrily.

"This is just any demon, Bastian. This is Amora, Valrick and Bronwyn's daughter," She informed.

"This is the half-demon, half-witch offspring?" He asked in surprise.

"Yes, she is," Nyra nodded. My form returned to normal except for my horns, which I guess had grown once more.

"I have a name, and it's not offspring," I muttered in irritation.

"I am very sorry, young lady," He apologized.

"Whatever," I grumbled.

"Let's not waste any more time out here, and we have urgent matters to get to," The man told us.

"Yes, we do," Nyra nodded. Nyra and I followed after the former Alpha King together.

Chapter Five

I sighed as we walked through the large main house of the Black Fang pack. The former Alpha King went straight to explaining the situation involving his pack. I tuned him out the entire time as we followed him through the house. As we walked through while the former Alpha King explained his pack's predicament, I stayed silent the whole time.

When we arrived at their hospital wing, I saw many people lying in beds, from infants to elderly members. A woman, who I assumed was the pack healer, walked towards us.

"How are things looking, Sarah?" he asked.

"Not good, sir. Everyone seems to have gotten worse, especially Marsha and John's son," she informed.

"It's a shame. He's only two months old," the former Alpha King sighed.

"I know, sir, but we've done everything we could to help him and everyone else as well," she sighed.

"I don't doubt that, Sarah," he nodded sadly. Sarah looked over at Nymphadora and me. When she saw me, she started growling defensively. I groaned and rolled my eyes.

"Ah, Sarah. This is Nyra. She came here to help us along with her companion Amora," he informed.

"Demons don't help anyone but themselves," she spat venomously.

"That's right, coming from a mere dog who just licks her ass," I spat, "Tell me, how much shit residue do you have just sat on your tongue?" Sarah growled at me again.

"Sarah, stand down," Bastian roared in his Alpha tone. Sarah stopped growling and merely glared at me. I smirked at her.

"Bastian, I won't apologize for my apprentice's behavior, for it was your pack member who started to antagonize her," Nyra told him.

"I'll make sure this doesn't happen again," Bastian nodded.

"Kid, give us the rundown on what's going on here," Nyra told the pack healer.

"I'll have you know that I am three hundred years old," The healer snapped.

"And I'll let you know I'm eight thousand years old. Now tell me what's going on now," Nyra responder. The healer started to explain what was going on with the members. As she explained, I began walking down the aisle, looking at each single-pack member lying in the hospital beds. As I was looking, something caught my eye about a child lying in a bed. I walked toward the child and noticed that dark purple boils covered half of his that looked painful to the touch. I walked towards the little boy, and I raised his arm. I closed my eyes and opened them quickly. My eyes turned pitch black as I scanned his body. I finally found what I was looking at. I stopped, and my eyes turned back to normal. I put a barrier around myself. I allowed my arms to begin turning black, my nails became black, my canines grew and sharpened, and my horns grew. I took one of my hands and stabbed it into the boy's chest. He gasped loudly, causing the healers, Bastian and Nyra, to look at me. The healers went into defensive mode along with the former Alpha King.

"Nyra! What is the meaning of this?!" he barked. I ignored them and continued what I was doing. I pulled out the boy's heart. Bastian shifted and charged at the barrier with his teeth bared. The little boy went still on the bed, and I looked at it. A demon had infected him and his pack members. I took one of my nails on my finger and dragged it down his heart. Bastian rammed his body against the barrier, and I could feel it starting to crack. The cut opened and raised his heart to my mouth, and I sucked out the poison infecting his body. His entire body began to heal as I continued to suck out the poison. His painful boils fell off his body and rolled onto the floor, turning into a black puddle. I healed the boy's heart with my magic and put it back into his chest. The hole sealed up just as Bastian broke the barrier completely. The little boy's body lifted off the bed as he gasped for breath. Bastian lunged at my throat, but I put him inside a bubble.

"Kill me, and your entire pack suffers, Bastian," I told him. He growled at me from inside the bubble.

"The feeling is mutual, you bastard," I hissed.

"Bastian, I'd prefer it if you'd quit trying to kill my apprentice over her healing method. It'd be a shame if your pack had to continue suffering once she's gone," Nyra spoke up. Bastian looked at me and growled again. He transformed into his human form, now naked, and glared evilly at me.

"Fine," he spat. I lowered the barrier.

"Nyra, I know who's causing this," I warned to the older woman.

"Alright. You know what to do," Nyra nodded. I froze time around us, causing Bastian and the rest of the world to freeze in place. I walked towards one of the healers, and I glared at her.

"Are you sure this is the right one?" She asked.

"There's no mistaking it. Demons who love to create and spread disease pose as healers or doctors, which makes them seem like unlikely suspects when things go wrong," I answered.

"Your knowledge of demons is awe-inspiring and very helpful as well," She remarked, "Your father would be impressed."

"Would be? I know he's impressed. The man lives to track my every move," I scoffed. She chuckled.

"That is true," She agreed. I looked at the healer and wrapped silver chains around her body. Sure enough, her skin began to sizzle. Demons, like vampires, couldn't stand silver. It was their own worst enemy. So, I knew that they would be in pure agony once I pressed play on time. I touched the demon on their forehead, and suddenly they fell to the floor, writhing in agony. They struggled against the chains that tightened.

"Curse you, you bitch!" The demon hissed.

"Yeah, yeah, yeah. Now take back the disease or else I'll melt one of these bad boys and pour it down your throat," I threatened.

"Never!" The demon hissed.

"Take it back now or else," I threatened harshly. The demon glared at me.

"Glare at me all you want, but you broke a rule in the demon kingdom: to leave this pack alone since I have a friend within this pack. You're lucky I'm dealing with you because if my father or anyone else had caught you, you would've been dead now. Now I'll repeat this, take back the disease, or else you'll suffer a fate worse than death," I snapped. The demon spat at me, and my eye started to burn.

"Fine. Since you want to do it the hard way, let me summon your king," I growled. The demon's eyes widened in fear.

"No, no, no! Wait," The demon rasped. The devil muttered an incantation that brought the entire disease he had spread around the pack back to himself. I smirked to myself.

"Nyra, it seems as if the big bad demon is a little scared," I remarked.

"Very scared," Nyra smiled. Once the disease completely disappeared, I unfroze time.

"Bastian," Nyra called out to the man. Bastian turned to look at us both.

"It seems like a demon was posing as a healer and spreading disease. As you can see, my apprentice and I have apprehended this demon, and we will properly deal with him," Nyra told him.

"Oh no, Nyra. He is on our land, and our terms shall deal with him," Bastian assured.

"We may be on your land, but this demon disobeyed my father, who brought immunity to this pack. This demon is my problem to deal for he is a subject of mine," I spoke up.

"A child should stay in a child's place," he spat.

"And a dog should stay in a dog's place," I hissed.

"Uncle, you ought to listen to her," I heard from behind us. I turned to see Eve walking into the room.

"The demon might've caused problems upon our land, but he also disobeyed his king. This demon is not our problem to deal with," Eve explained, "He is the demon king's, and I don't think we should intervene."

"Know your place, Eve," He snapped in an Alpha tone.

" I'm sorry, sir," Eve held her head down. I knew that she couldn't do anything about considering how this was her former Alpha, but that didn't mean it didn't piss me off any less.

"You're getting on my fucking nerves," I hissed. I flicked my wrist over the demon, and silver started to come from the ground up and encase its body like a hard shell. The demon hissed and screamed in agony like a wounded animal. Bastian glared at me hatefully. After surrounding the devil, the silver turned to ash on the floor.

"There. The problem is dealt with," I snapped, "Nyra, I'm going home."

Chapter Six

o you realize how irresponsibly dangerous it was for you to provoke Bastian, a former Alpha King?" my mother yelled at me.

"Do you realize how irresponsible he was to be that much of an asshole?" I shot at her. My mother glared at me, and I soon felt my arms forced behind my back. My hands clasped together, and soon I felt the horrible burning sensation of silver chains on my wrists. I cried out in pain and dropped down to one knee.

"Curse at me again, and you'll get an ass whooping that'll sting worse than those chains," She hissed.

"Y-yes....m-ma'am," I struggled.

"One thing you need to remember is that when it comes to affairs that involve different supernatural beings, you abide by their rules, Amora. Nyra, Alan, your father, and I didn't waste years of training you and teaching you just for you to forget that. Honestly, had I not talked Bastian down from punishing you for treason against his pack, then you wouldn't be standing here today," My Mom explained.

"That....demon....that...bastard...was...was...going to....to.... harm Eve," I wearied. The chains slipped my wrists and onto the floor. When it comes to silver, my powers, from my witch side and my demonic ones, were weakened, and I was also physically drained because my abilities tied me to my life force. My mother sighed and kneeled beside me.

"I know you were trying to help, sweetie, but you have to realize that there are some things you can and can't do. You can't just go around making rash decisions like your idiot father," She explained.

"You have to be careful, and you have to be mindful of the consequences of your actions," she said.

"Fine," I muttered.

"Now, Bastian's son messaged me last night, and he's not pleased. Like his father, he wants to see you punished for your actions. I've tried talking him down, but he doesn't seem the talking," she informed me.

"So, what does that mean?" I asked.

"That means that you're going to take your ass back to that packhouse, and you're going to apologize to him in exactly a month," She explained.

"Why a month?" I questioned.

"He was on business for three months in Europe checking on the other packs within that area. As the new Alpha King, he has an enormous responsibility like your father and me, which will soon be passed on to you," she answered.

"Mom, why can't I just be both a supreme and a demon queen?" I asked.

"Because you can only choose one and one only," She replied

"Fine," I sighed loudly.

"As much as I would love to force you into my position, I simply can't because it's your choice to decide whether you want to lead this coven or the demon world. You can choose both because both positions require you to give them your full and undivided attention," Mom explained.

"And what if I just say I don't want either?" I asked.

"Then your father and I will put you in a stone tomb wrapped in silver chains for eternity until you decide," She answered.

"That's child abuse," I squinted my eyes.

"Eh. It's called helping," She shrugged.

"Now, since you have one month until you meet the Alpha King, you'll be training extra hard every day with Nymphadora and Alan," She informed me.

"What?!" I exclaimed.

"This is your punishment for being irrationally stupid," She replied, "Now run along." I groaned and stood on shaky legs. I whistled a broomstick toward me, sat on it, and looked at my mother.

"Have fun, and don't forget about your meeting," She smiled.

"Yes, Mother," I mumbled. She kissed my forehead and then stepped back. She waved to me, and soon the broom was zooming out of her house. I arrived at my usual training spot and found Alan and Nyra waiting for me. I stepped off the broom, and I almost fell to the ground.

"I heard about your little conflict with that mutt Bastian. I can't say I'm proud," Alan chastised. I held my head down.

"I can't say that I'm proud because you didn't kill the damn dog," he growled.

"Had she harmed that man in any way, his son, the new king, would've gone after her head and even waged war on our coven," Nyra snapped, "Although you demons would love for an all-out war to happen, you need to at least think about how Valrick would feel if that happened. His nature and protecting his mate and child would tear at him." Alan glared at her for a moment, then looked away.

"Let's get this damn training over with," He grumbled.

"Yes. Let's," Nyra agreed.

"I'm still weak from being chained earlier. Can we hold on a second?" I asked.

"If a pair of small chains around your wrists makes you weak, then no, we won't 'hold on,'" Alan snapped.

"Shit," I muttered under my breath.

"You're still far too. You have to build up your strength so that small chains don't weaken you entirely," he told me.

"So, what does that mean?" I questioned.

"That means you will build yourself up each day by having a small silver cuff on your wrist. You will not be allowed to take it off, nor will you be allowed to ask someone else to take it off," He explained, "Your father had gone through these same methods when he was in training, and so shall you." I nodded. Alan walked over to me with a metal cuff in his hand. He put it around my wrist, and I soon felt it begin to burn. I felt myself getting weak again.

"Now, let's commence this training session," he ordered. I nodded.

"Your father told me not to go easy on you today due to your transgressions," he smirked. "I don't plan on holding back on you in your weakened state, so don't expect me to be sympathetic."

"Funny, and Bronwyn said the same thing," Nyra spoke up behind me.

"Great mates think alike," Alan remarked.

"Yes, they do," Nyra grinned maliciously. They both turned to me, and I sighed to myself. This was going to be a long day.

Chapter Seven

was currently visiting my father in Nazareth for two days or two weeks in the mundane world. Two days turned into two weeks in the ordinary world I live because time runs differently here. A day here in Nazareth turns into a week there, a week here turns into a month there, a month here turns into a year there, and a year here turns into a century there. Because of this, I had to be careful about how long I stayed here because when I was fifteen and still going to human school, I stayed with my father for three days and ended up missing three weeks. The school had gone crazy, and one of my teachers, that nosy and crazy bitch, had called the police on my mother and made up a damn story that she had possibly murdered me or something. Mind you; this teacher only said that because she had a thing for my dad and wanted to get with him at any cost. The police had taken my mom in for investigation about my 'disappearance' and even tried to charge her with manslaughter, but that was until my dad intervened with me in tow and told them that I had been spending time with him. The officers got suspicious again and tried to arrest my dad on some made-up charges because they wanted to date my mom. Long story short, the whole ordeal was just crazy anyway because people let their personal feelings get in the way of their jobs. My parents agreed that I could only stay with my dad on holidays since he had to live in Nazareth full-time. So, I only stayed with my dad during the summer and my mom during the school year, which worked because I got to spend more time with my dad, my abuela, and my abuelo.

I used my visit to Nazareth as an excuse to stay away from the mundane world until I had to apologize. My dad kept track so I wouldn't miss my responsibility and even reminded me. However, my grandparents didn't even like that I had to apologize because they felt I shouldn't have had to apologize. My dad had to keep telling them I was obligated to do so because I had overstepped my boundaries on their land. My grandparents still argued that I shouldn't be with my dad and spoiled me rotten like every grandparent in the world does. My grandmother cooked more food for me than was necessary, and my grandfather gave me many valuable jewels plus some great life advice.

"I can't believe you'll be leaving us tomorrow," My abuela sighed.

"I know, abuela. I'll miss you too," I hugged her.

"It's so lovely having you here, mi preciosa nieta," She smiled softly, “I know you have your training and all to become the next supreme or the next demon queen, but I wish you'd visit more often. Your grandfather and I aren't getting any younger, and your father isn’t either."

"I promise to visit more, abuela," I murmured.

"I'll be looking forward to it, nieta," She smiled. I hugged her again, and she kissed my cheek.

"Now, how does trying on that dress I had tailored for your sound?" She asked.

"Is it Red, abuela?" I questioned.

"Red as the blood that runs through the veins of those humans," She replied. I chuckled.

"I'm in. I have been dying to see this dress since you told me about it," I smiled.

"I just know you'll love it, especially considering how your taste in clothes comes from me," she grinned. I giggled.

"They sure do, abuela. They sure do," I sighed happily.

The following day, the day I was leaving, had come. I was now dreading going home. I honestly wanted to stay here forever and be spoiled, more like fattened up, by my grandparents. Still, my mother sent me a message last night saying that if I didn't come home and fulfill my duty, she would skin me alive and make me walk around with all my important organs and muscles out in the open for the world to see. So, I knew that hiding out here wasn't an option. Complying with my mother was my best option because I didn't want to feel her wrath after I disobeyed her.

"You have everything right, nieta?" My grandmother asked worriedly.

"Sí, abuela," I nodded.

"You sure?" She questioned.

"I am. Don't worry. I'll come back and visit you guys as soon as this ordeal ends," I assured her.

"Promise?" She questioned.

"Prometo en mi vida eterna," I responded.

"Te amo, mi hermosa nieta," She mumbled as she pulled me into a hug.

"Yo también te amo, abuela " I hugged her back. She kissed my cheek again. I turned to my abuelo, standing next to my grandmother with a warm smile on his face.

"Now, if those dogs give you hell, then make sure you call me so I can show them how we Rodríguez, hombres y mujeres, manejan perros," he told me. I giggled.

"I'll be sure to do that, abuelo," I smiled.

"If that brat Bastian gives you any more trouble, then tell him to 'recuerda la batalla del infierno'," he told me.

"Abuelo, what's that?" I asked in confusion.

"Nothing you should concern yourself with, nieta, but saying that to him will get him to wise up," My grandfather responded.

"Alright, Abuelo," I nodded. He kissed my forehead and murmured that he would miss me in Spanish. I stepped towards my dad, who was standing a few yards away. My grandparents waved to me, and I waved back.

"Ready?" My dad asked.

"As I'll ever be, padre," I responded.

"Good," He grinned, and his sharp canines showed, "Let's go." He snapped his fingers, and instantly we were engulfed in a warm and brilliant orange flame. Soon we were transported back to my mother's house, where she was waiting for us. My mom completely ignored my dad and walked toward me.

"Amora, I'm so glad you're back," She hugged me.

"It's great to be back, Mom," I smiled.

"You'll have to tell me how your visit went later, but first, I need you to go upstairs and shower. I need you to get dressed so we can head to the Black Fang pack house. The Alpha King arrived last night, and he's getting impatient by the second," she told me.

"Yes, Mom," I nodded. I turned to my dad.

"I'll see you later, Padre," I hugged him.

"You too, Lani," He kissed my forehead. He turned to mother and took her hand into his, kissing the back of it.

"Por favor háblame otra vez, mi hermosa esposa," He murmured lovingly to her. Her face softened, and she looked at him.

"Lani, go upstairs and get ready. Your father and I have some things to discuss," she said. I nodded and headed upstairs as told.

My mother and I arrived together outside the Black Fang pack's house. I dreaded even coming here in the first place because a) I didn't want to be at this shit hole any longer, b) I could care less about their rules, and c) they could all go fuck themselves. One thing I didn't understand about this visit was that I had to change into something more 'decent' in my mother's eyes. I didn't understand it because my clothing choices were decent. I guess wearing sweatpants and a sweatshirt to apologize to someone is just too 'disrespectful.' I honestly wasn't going to waste a nice outfit on them, yet I was in a lovely ensemble of mine, standing outside their house. Currently, I was wearing an olive-green sleeveless dress, a pair of black thigh-high boots, and an oversized denim jacket.

"I can't believe I let you talk me into letting you wear that," She shook her head.

"You told me to look decent, and so I gave you decent," I replied as we talked towards the gate.

"Decent as in business casual or something, Amora," she said.

"Well, it's too late. I don't feel like changing, Mom," I said.

"Ugh. One of these days, I swear you're going to make me bring down a whole forest," She groaned.

"The day you do that is the day grandmother will rise from her eternal slumber and choke you," I remarked.

"I hate it when you're right," She grumbled. We both stopped in front of the gate together.

"Since you're the one who's apologizing, I can't go with you because this problem is yours to handle. My hands are tied," She sighed.

"I know, Mom," I replied.

"All I can say now is good luck," She told me, "Remember not to get an attitude and remember to keep that temper of yours in check."

"I will, Mom," I nodded.

"Alright, Amora. I'll be waiting at home for you," She informed me.

"Okay, Mom," I responded.

"And make sure you fill me in on what happens when this is over," she said.

"I promise Mom," I replied. She hugged me and kissed my forehead.

"Good luck, be safe, and don't let your guard down," she said.

"I won't," I assured her. She smiled softly and stepped away from me. Soon she was engulfed in a flurry of leaves. The leaves dropped to the ground as soon as she was gone. I looked toward the house, and I breathed in deeply. I walked towards it quickly. I wanted to get this shit over and done with already. When I reached the door, I raised my hand to knock, but the door swung open to reveal two big burly guys. Before I could speak, I was grabbed and pulled inside. The guys gripped my arms tightly.

"Hey! This shit fucking hurts!" I snapped. They ignored me and continued to drag me down the hallway roughly. Members of the pack glared at me and snarled as they dragged me down the hallway. I struggled against those guys' unbreakable hold. I can see why Alan hates wolves. They were mongrels who thought with their muscles instead of their brains. I was led down a long hallway with two large double doors at the end. When we reached the doors, they dropped me to the floor, and I groaned in pain. I became angry that these brutes had done that to me. I turned to look at them both, and I bared my teeth. They growled back at me, but I cut that shit off by clenching my hand. Both men dropped to their knees as they gasped for air. I stood up and looked down at them.

"Let that be a lesson to you so that next time you won't feel my wrath," I snapped. I cut off their air supply with my magic until they passed out. I smirked and then turned around, only to find myself face-to-face with a hard chest. Shit. I slowly looked up and into the piercing blue eyes of the Alpha King. I started to feel a warm sensation come over me as I stood there. It wasn't an uncomfortable warmth, but it was a hot and inviting warmth. I soon felt a slight tugging in my heart as I looked at this man. Oh no. Oh no. Oh no. Oh no. Uh-uh. This shit can't be happening. I heard a low growl, and I looked at Alpha King. I saw his blue eyes flickering between blue and a blueish-white color.

"Mine," He growled possessively. Yep. I had found my mate. Like any reasonable person, who had just seen her mate, I turned to run away, which failed because he had wrapped his arms around my waist and pulled me into him. Damn it. I should've made a portal or something.

"Let me go!" I snapped. He said nothing as he carried me through the large double doors as I thrashed against him. Because he wouldn't let go, I leaned my head down and bit him hard on the arm. He yelped and let go of me. In my expert opinion, it wasn't a good idea in the first place to bite the guy who was carrying me, but I needed some way to have him let me go. He growled in anger and grabbed me. He threw me into the chair and had his pack members restrain me.

"Let me go!" I hissed. He glared at me as he took a seat at his desk

"I'm not going to do that," he said.

"What?! Why?" I hissed as I thrashed in their grip.

"You may be my mate, but you broke the rules of the treaty, which was to never interfere with the matters on any other supernatural's land," He told me.

"I'm sorry for overstepping my bounds. Now let me go!" I snapped.

"I'm afraid I cannot do that," he said.

"And why not?" I asked angrily.

"Even if you are my mate, you deserve punishment for your transgressions," He responded.

"What?! You said all I had to do was apologize!" I seethed.

"Your apology would've meant nothing either way. You need to face the consequences of your actions," He sneered.

"The fuck? You trick me!" I growled.

"No, and I simply left out the punishment part," He smirked.

"You're a fucking bastard!" I fumed.

"Takes one to know one," He countered. I tried breaking out of the hold of his lackeys, but they were too strong.

"For your punishment, I will send you to our dungeon for three days, where you will starve," he informed me.

"You can't do this to me!" I yelled. He walked around the desk and looked down at me smugly.

"I can and I will because you are on my land," he said. I used my magic to transform into a shadow and dart quickly. I would not allow him to lock me away for three days. Some day that bastard is going to get what's coming to him, but I can't believe that I, Amora Isabelle Rodríguez, have found my mate, the guy I'm supposed to apologize to for the shit I did. Ugh! Why me? Just why? I can't fucking believe this. I don't want a mate. I've never wanted a mate in the first place, but I can't just reject the guy because that would be the most disgraceful thing in the world, especially in the world of us supernaturals.

I managed to get away from their land as quickly as possible, and as soon as I got to a clearing, I made a portal to my mother's home. I walked towards my mother's house, and I headed inside. She looked at me curiously.

"That was fast. Did you apologize?" She asked.

"No," I shook my head.

"What?! Amora!" She exclaimed.

"Mom, if you had been, then you would've known there was no time for me to apologize after what had just happened," I told her.

"What could've possibly happened that stopped you from apologizing?" She questioned.

"I found my mate," I informed her.

"What?! That's great, sweetie," She smiled.

"No, it's not, Mom," I shook my head.

"And why isn't it great?" She questioned.

"My mate is the Alpha King," I replied.

"Whaaaaaaaaat?!" She looked at me in surprise.

8

Chapter Eight

Usually supernatural creatures would jump for joy because they found their mate. As for me, I wasn't jumping, nor was I doing it for pleasure. I can't fucking believe that out of all the supernatural creatures in the world; I was mated to the Alpha King. Ain't that some shit, to be honest. The guy was a total and complete douchebag. I wanted nothing more than to choke him until he passed out, wrap his body in chains, put him inside a stone tomb, wrap chains around the grave, make a circle around it with wolfsbane, and seal the entrance to the tomb with wolfsbane. That way, I don't have to deal with him anymore, and he won't be able to escape his prison. It's an elaborate plan, I know, but I couldn't stand the guy no matter what. He was such a fucking meathead.

Because he was my mate, Eve and the rest of her pack members found out through a mind link. Eve was jumping for joy because now we were family, her mother and father were happy, and her aunt and uncle were also disgusted. I honestly couldn't be careless about what her aunt and uncle thought because they could suck my dick and choke on it. As for my parents, my mom was excited that I found my mate because she thought, and I quote, that I would 'be a lonely old lady who would walk this earth for eternity with Salem by my side.' On the other hand, my dad was happy but not too comfortable because he hated wolves. He couldn't stand them, even though he liked Eve, and he wanted nothing more than for me to reject him. My abuela and abuelo agreed with him. Nyra, however, was neutral about the situation. She just told me to do whatever made me happy and left it. Alan was more upset because he couldn't stand wolves like my father and grandparents. He just couldn't.

Currently, it's been two weeks since I found out who my mate was, and I am hiding in Nazareth. Eve has been texting me to come back every day that she was in the mundane and telling me that hiding from my mate was the worst idea in the world. I replied, telling her that I didn't give a damn if hiding was the worst idea because the moment he set foot in this realm would be the last time he'd ever be alive.

"This entire predicament reminds me of when your mother and I discovered we were mates. I remember how she kept running from me for centuries because she was afraid to be mates with me. It was a little comical to see her running from me, but it was worth the chase," He smirked, "It was especially worth it when I finally caught her."

"Dad, ew! I don't want to hear that!" I exclaimed.

"Well, that is what brought you into this world," He chuckled.

"It's still gross to hear your parents talking about it," I responded. He laughed again.

"I will say this," he told me.

"What?" I asked.

"You and the rest of the Driscoll women have been known for centuries to run away from your mates," He informed me.

"Really?" I turned to him.

"Yes. Your grandmother Agatha told me about it before she went into her eternal sleep. She told me that the Driscoll women were known for running away from their mates for centuries. She says that your strong independence passed down from generation to generation makes you all so reluctant even to want a mate," He explained.

"Oh wow. I never knew that," I mumbled.

"Your grandfather, may his soul rest eternally, told me stories of how your grandmother would run to the ends of the earth just to get away from him, but he always managed to find her no matter what, and it pissed her off badly," He chuckled.

"Did Mom feel the same way?" I asked.

"She did. One time I was chasing her, and I caught her; she had struck me harshly with her magic. It left a deep and permanent scar right here," My dad lowered the collar of his shirt.

"Did she apologize?" I questioned.

"She did for centuries and continued to do so after you were born. Even though we were not speaking for years, she still found moments when you weren't paying attention to apologize. It makes me fall in love with your mother more and more every day to know that she loves and cares for me," He replied.

"Speaking of you guys' falling out, are you two on better terms?" I questioned.

"We're getting there, but it's hard to communicate when we both have obligations to need our full attention," He sighed, "Especially you." I smiled softly.

"I wish you guys didn't fight over something like this," I sighed.

"Me too, but you have to see it our way. Your mother and I are rulers of our people, and we are obligated to have an heir that will take over our responsibilities. Life would be much easier had your mother and I been able to create another child, so we could groom them to become the next demon queen or the next supreme. At least you won't have such a huge burden on yourself to choose," He explained. I never really saw it that way, and now that I do, I started to feel a little bad.

"So, how long do you plan on staying here?" He asked.

"Considering how I'm a fugitive, I plan on staying a month," I informed.

"A year in your time? Really?" He questioned.

"Yeah. When he found out I was his mate, the guy told me it didn't matter and that an apology wouldn't suffice after what I did. He wanted to keep me locked away in a dungeon for three days where he would starve me," I explained.

"What?!" My dad yelled angrily.

"Oh snap. I forgot to mention that part," I mumbled.

"He told your mother and me that you were going to apologize, and he deceived us," My dad hissed. Oh shit. The Alpha King might be my mate, but that doesn't mean my dad won't kill him.

"I'm telling your mother, and the both of us are going to that packhouse because you do not sit here and deceive me, the demon king, nor do you deceive my mate, the supreme," His voice became more demonic as he spoke. The entire realm started to shake. My dad was so angry that he transformed into a horrifyingly scary form that would give the average human nightmares for years. His form even gave me nightmares when I was five that lasted until I was ten. After he saw how badly his demonic form had scared me when I was a child, my dad never showed it to me; even now, he doesn't show it to me, nor does he show it to my mother. He's told us in the past that he doesn't want us to see him in that form and that seeing him that way was not something he wanted.

"Dad, please calm down," I pleaded.

"No! That bastard dared to deceive me, and he dared to harm you! I will not tolerate this!" He yelled.

"Dad-" I reached out for him, but suddenly he stomped the ground, and I was unexpectedly blown backward into a wall. Pain shot up my back, as I said, embedded in the stone walls of my father's castle. I groaned. I managed to get myself out of the wall and groaned again. I looked at where my father once was, and black ash covered the ground. Shit. Now I got to save my asshole of a mate. Great. Just fucking great

Chapter Nine

After my dad had left, I wasted no time leaving. I told my grandparents that I would be back, and they understood. I managed to use my magic to create a portal to get to my mother's house. She was the only one who could calm my dad down before he destroyed something. When I arrived at her house, I noticed wolves standing outside it like a patrol or something. They all saw me and started to come towards me.

"I don't have time for this!" I yelled. I froze them all in place and walked towards the house.

"Mom! Mom! We have a problem!" I yelled to her as I rose from the ground.

"My alpha predicted that you would pop up here," I heard from behind. I turned to see a huge guy with short brown hair, bulging muscle, a jawline for days, brown eyes, and a frame that stood at 6'1 behind me.

"I don't have time for you either," I snapped. I froze him in place and turned to my mom.

"What happened, Amora?" She asked worriedly.

"I told Dad about how the Alpha King lied about me giving an apology and how he wanted to imprison me. Now he's angry and about to burn the place down," I replied.

"You told him about what Jayden did, didn't you?" She frowned.

"Jayden? Who the hell is Jayden?" I scrunched my eyebrows in confusion.

"How the hell do you have a mate and not know his name?" She asked.

"Between me wanting to kill him myself and not giving a damn is how I don't know his name or let alone want to know it," I responded.

"Wait. We're getting off track," she said.

"Yeah, we are, and we need to—"

"LANI!" Eve burst into the house, "I got your message! Let's go!" I notified Eve as soon as I arrived. She was just as scared about what my dad might do to her cousin as I was, and I wasn't all that worried anyway.

"All this time we spent talking, and we could've used it trying to get there," My Mom said. A gust of wind blew into the house, and I closed my eyes as I embraced what was about to happen. I was outside the Black Fang pack house with my mom and Eve when I opened them. I looked at the home and noticed the front of the house had been blasted open.

"He's here alright," My Mom remarked. Eve transformed into her wolf, and I changed as well. My mom, Eve, and I walked towards the house together.

"Eve, go check to see if anyone got hurt," My Mom said. Eve nodded and ran off.

"As for you, Amora, I want you to locate your mate. Your father is going to be wherever he is," she told me. I nodded. Locating people was easy, especially if I got their scent down. Even though my encounter with him was brief and crazy as fuck, I knew what he smelled like. He had a powerful yet indescribable scent that sent my hormones into overdrive, meaning that his scent made me horny. His scent was part of why I didn't even want him as a mate because it made me horny. I'll admit that I contemplated whether I wanted to jump his bones or kill him the first time I met him.

I had finally found him. He was out back in the woods behind the house. I grabbed my mom by the wrist and transported us there. When we arrived in the woods, I saw him with blood on his face next to a tree. My dad was getting ready to strike him down. A robust and palm-sized barrier formed in my hand. I hope this works. I threw it at my dad, and it instantly went around him. My Dad growled in anger and turned to my mother and me.

"Valrick! Calm the fuck down!" My Mother yelled. Jayden raises his head to look at me. He growled at me angrily.

"He deceived us, Bronwyn," He hissed.

"I know that, and I'll deal with him in another way," She told him.

"He tried to hurt my little girl. I cannot allow that," He snapped.

"I know, honey, but killing him won't solve anything," She said, "Killing him will only bring more problems." My Dad looked at my mom and then sighed. He started turning back to his human form.

"I won't kill him for you, Bronwyn," He promised, "However if he dares to lay a finger on my little girl, I will not hesitate to strike him down." I walked over to Jayden as my dad glared at him, and he looked up at me and growled.

"Listen, you can get angry all you want, but technically you brought this upon yourself," I snapped, "But I apologize for what I did. I overstepped my boundaries, so there. You got your apology, you bastard. Now, after today, you will leave me the fuck alone, or else you'll have to deal with my father again, and believe me, that's something you don't want to do again. Understand?" He glared at me but nodded.

"Good. Now let's head back to your pack house so I can heal you," I told him, "And you might want to transform first." He complied again and went into his human form.

"Lani, your father and I will see you later," My mother said. My mom was standing next to my dad, glaring hard at Jayden.

"Okay," I nodded.

"Be safe," She replied.

"I will," I smiled.

"Oh, Jayden," My Mother said.

"Yes?" He hissed. My dad glared even harder at him.

"Yes, Bronwyn?" He spoke.

"Welcome to the family," She replied. With a crack, her and my father disappeared.

"I'd rather not be in this damn family," He growled.

"You have no choice, considering how if you reject me, you'll never find a mate again. You'll be a lone wolf who will never produce an heir that will take over your position as Alpha King. I suggest you suck it up and deal with it," I hissed. He growled at me again, and I snapped my fingers. A muzzle appeared on his face. He tried wrenching it from his face, but it was no use.

"Now come on, mate," I smirked.

~*~

"It is highly disrespectful towards me that you guys would even force me to freak move in with a man I loathe entirely," I grumbled to my Mother and Nyra. It had been three months since that incident at the Black Fang Pack House, and things between Jayden and me, relationship-wise, had gotten worse. That means that we totally and utterly hated each other passionately, even though we were mates. I still wanted to kill the guy, but that meant starting a war I wouldn't be interested in fighting in because I would kill the entire pack, except for Eve and her parents. It's a little harsh, I know, but that's just how I felt.

"Well, you two are mates who hate each other's guts, and that's not normal at all," Mother said.

"No, it isn't, which means that if you guys move in together and share a bed, then maybe, just maybe, you'll both have growing feelings for each other," Nyra explained.

"Or growing feelings of hatred that will lead me to smother him in his sleep or possibly drown him," I responded.

"You will do no such thing because I will monitor your activity every morning to see if you haven't killed the boy yet," Mother scolded. I groaned loudly.

"Well, why would you force us both to live in a huge house by ourselves on their property?" I questioned.

"Because his parents only agreed to this arrangement because they wanted to be able to know where their son is at all times," Mother informed me.

"And you couldn't just decline the offer because...?" I looked at her.

"Because I didn't want to get into it with those two about this shit, plus Bastian's mate pisses me off with her young ass," Mother replied.

"How does she make you upset?" I questioned.

"She thinks that because her ass got the title of Alpha Queen that she's above everyone else, which isn't true anyways, considering how she doesn't have any political knowledge at all, and she doesn't care to have political knowledge at all. She's just a dumb bimbo with a title," Mother explained. I chuckled.

"I remember two hundred years ago when Bastian first got his title as Alpha King, I asked her about her stance on the rising tensions between the King of the Fae and the King of the Vampires. Do you know what she told me?" Mother questioned.

"What?" I asked.

"She told me that she honestly didn't give a damn because it wasn't her problem and didn't affect her. This dumb ass bitch thought that, and it pissed me off because the King of the Fae has close ties to her husband. The King of the Vampires has had a peace treaty with the wolves since 1604. If the Vampires And Fae had gone to war, then many of us supernaturals would've picked a side, which meant that that war would've been ugly and very devastating to not only us supernaturals but the humans as well. She didn't think about that and didn't care to think because she's a dumb bitch!" Mother informed me.

I looked at her in shock. I was astonished at how she was talking because I'd never seen her this angry, but I could understand her anger. Someone who doesn't take the time to learn about politics or care to learn about it in the world of supernaturals was an ignoramus. My mother, father, abuela, abuelo, Alan, Salem, and Nyra taught me all the basics. She even had me sit in on some meetings, like the Council of Supernaturals, which hands royalty from many different species of supernaturals there.

"What pisses me off is that she'll sit in on our meetings and say some dumb shit at the same time," Mother ranted. I looked at Nyra, who just shook her head. I guess I was going just to let my mother yell.

An hour later, she was helping me pack again when she finished. My entire bedroom at Nyra's was bare, leaving only my bed, dresser, and bookshelf. I packed my things into three large trunks. As for the things I use to create potions and magic circles, they were placed into a large enough case to fit all of it, and there was a lot.

"There. That should be it," Mother smiled.

"Great," I mumbled.

"Oh, come on. It won't be so bad," Mother said.

"Believe me, it will be so bad," I muttered.

"Think of the bright side. At least you'll get to see Eve every day," Mother added.

"I love Eve, but seeing her every single day still won't make it any better," I responded.

"You can't forget Michelle's famous brownies," she said.

"Her brownies?" I asked.

"I knew that would get her," Mother murmured to Nyra. Nyra chuckled.

"I forgot to say that not only will I be monitoring you, but Eve's father, Harrison, will come and check in on you guys every single day," She informed me, "That way, he can report to me on if you two have caused each other harm in any way."

"This is starting to sound more like a prison sentence with every passing second," I remarked.

"She's right, you know," Salem spoke up as she walked into the room.

"Salem, where have you been?" I questioned.

"Oh, I've been away on business for your mother," She answered.

"Okay," I nodded.

"As for this arrangement, I can monitor those two for you. There's no need to bother Harrison about it anyways. Michelle has told me that Harrison has been catching a lot of flack, especially from his brother and his mate. Harrison already has enough to deal with as is. There's no need to worry him about checking in on your daughter and her boneheaded mate," Salem explained.

"Mr. H is getting in trouble because of me?" I asked.

"Yes, and so is Eve as well. The members of their pack have shunned them in a sense for being associated with you," She replied.

"Those bastards," I growled. I felt my horns start to make their appearance out of my head. My nails began to grow and turn black, my arms turned black with red veins, my canines elongated and sharpened on both rows of my teeth, my tongue became long with a pointed tip, my eyes blackened, and I felt spikes rip my clothing on my shoulders. Now the points growing out of my shoulders were new. I discovered this a month ago. I guess I was starting to become more demon than anything.

"Amora, calm down," Mother said.

"How can I when they're treating Eve and her parents like trash," I hissed.

"I know it's bad, honey, but you have to understand that getting angry won't help anything at all," She told me.

"Getting angry will help because then I'll show them my wrath," I snapped.

"Showing them your wrath will cause more problems for Ever and her parents. You have to realize that, Amora," Nyra told me.

"So what am I supposed to do? Allow them to treat her this way?" I asked.

"No, but you must sit down and have a civilized conversation with your mate. You need to tell him that you will not tolerate the pack members' mistreatment of Eve and her parents," Nyra explained. I soon calmed down, and my features returned to normal except for the horns, which I groaned. It took me a month to get them to retract, and now they were back.

"Fine. I'll talk to the bastard about it, but I won't like it," I growled as I used my magic to stitch my clothes back together.

"That's the spirit. Now put on your shoes so we can go," Mother told me. Nyra touched my trunks, causing them to disappear, and I knew she had sent them to my new 'home.' My mother, Nyra, and Salem walked out of my room. I slipped on my sneakers, and I stood up. I looked around my room and my childhood bedroom and sighed.

"Goodbye," I sighed.

10

Chapter Ten

Salem, my mother, Nyra, and I stood outside of my new home. I scrunched my nose up in disgust.

"Tell me again why we agreed to this," I spoke up.

"Because you and your mate need to get to know each other. It's time you and I broke this tradition of women of the Driscoll family running away from our mates because we value our independence too much," She explained.

"Ugh! Why can't we live on the land for the coven? Why do we have to live here?" I groaned.

"Because this was the only way his parents would agree," She said.

"Agree? I wouldn't give a rat's booty hole if they disagreed. We should've stayed on the land of the coven," I replied. My cheek was suddenly grabbed and pulled.

"Considering how someone's negotiating skills are as bad as a Vikings, I'd say that I did us all a favor by doing this," She snapped.

"Ow! Ow! Ow! Ow!" I exclaimed. She grabbed my other cheek and pulled.

"Since you seem to love talking about what you 'should do,' you should get inside that damn house and suck it up before I beat you with my broomstick!" She hissed.

"Owwwwwww!" I exclaimed.

"Worse than your damn father with all that complaining and shit," She fumed, "And I had to deal with that shit for a thousand years." She let go of my face, and I rubbed my cheeks. I scowled at the ground because I knew glaring at her would lead to more pain.

"Now come on so we can put your things away," She told me. I followed them wordlessly. When we reached the house, we all went inside. I saw my trunks sitting near the door and put them beside each other. I flicked my wrist, and the boxes flew open.

"We each take a trunk," Mother informed us. Nyra and I nodded. Salem walked over to the large living room to lie on a chair in the corner of the room. We each snapped our fingers, and my things started floating out of my chest and placing themselves in their new designated spots in the house. Once I finished everything, we carried my trunks to a medium-sized coat closet and put them in there.

"We've finished our work here, so Nyra and I will be heading out," Mother informed me.

"What? Why?" I asked.

"Because we have somewhere to be, and helping you get here and unpack was all we were going to do," She answered.

"So you're leaving me all alone within this house?" I questioned.

"Pretty much, kid. Have fun," Nyra smiled, and she disappeared with a crack. Mother chuckled and walked over to kiss me on the forehead.

"See you later, my baby," She smiled. She, too, disappeared with a crack. Great. All alone in this big stupid house, Salem was here, but she was sleeping. I guess I can go check out my new bed, and I mean sleep. I walked up the stairs to the new bedroom I had now shared with Jayden. I walked towards one of the dressers and opened it. I saw that my pajamas and other things were in there. I stripped off my clothes until I was down to my bra and under. I pulled on an oversized t-shirt and picked up my clothes to put them in the hamper. When I finished, I climbed into the cool bed and very comfortable bed before drifting off into a deep sleep.

~*~

I awoke several hours later and noticed it was dark outside. I sat in bed and yawned as I scratched my stomach. Swinging my legs over the bed, I stood up and walked out of the bedroom. As

I was about to descend the stairs and noticed a light was on downstairs. Too tired to even feel like killing whoever the intruder was, I sniffed the air. There were two scents in this house that I recognized. One was a lavender scent, and the other was one that I've said was indescribable. I knew the lavender odor was Salem, and I guess the other was Jayden. I walked downstairs into the kitchen and found Salem perched on a railing.

"I was wondering when you would wake up," She said.

"How long have you been awake?" I questioned.

"I woke up an hour ago when Prince Charming over there arrived," She replied.

"More like Prince Douchebag," I mumbled. I heard growling and knew he had heard us, but my I-Don't-Give-A-Shit-itis was acting up again. I rolled my eyes and turned to Salem.

"What would you like for dinner?" I asked.

"What do you feel like cooking?" She inquired.

"I was thinking more like steak," I responded.

"Grilled or broiled?" She questioned.

"Broiled for sure," I answered.

"That could work," She nodded.

"What kind of sides do you feel like eating?" I queried.

"Hm. How about asparagus and mashed potatoes?" She questioned.

"That sounds good," I nodded. Salem hopped off the railing and onto the floor. She followed me into the kitchen, where Jayden was along with his beta, delta, and gamma. I ignored them and headed straight for the sink, where I washed my hands. I headed to the freezer and took out the steak pack with only two. It was a little frozen, but that was nothing that a little heat couldn't fix. Salem hopped onto the counter and sat there, and I put a soundproof barrier around us so we could talk.

"So what did you have to do that involves you being away for a while?" I asked. I produced a flame on the palm of my hand, and I started to defrost the meat.

"I had to go talk to the King of Wyverns. Your mother wanted to discuss with him the possibility of joining your clans as allies," She explained.

"Allies with Wyverns? I thought they had been adamant about not wanting to become allies with us," I replied.

"They were, but after negotiating with them and promising them protection, they agreed," She informed.

"Aren't the Wyverns also allies with my father?" I asked as I finished defrosting the meat.

"They are, but they have your mother a harder time considering how she's a woman," Salem truthfully stated.

"Men," I rolled my eyes. Even in the supernatural world, women were still being discriminated against, especially if they were in places of power. It's a little infuriating, but it was true. This shows you that no matter what species you are if you're a woman, you'll always be overlooked or disrespected by men.

"I can't wait until the other children of these old rulers come into power," I murmured, "I feel like the supernatural world will be much better for us women."

"Funny how your Mother said the same thing," She remarked.

"Really?" I asked with a small smile.

"Yes. She believes that once the children of rulers like her and your father will claim your birthright, then you'll all make it possible for no supernatural creature not to feel left out or discriminated against," She answered.

"Like mother, like daughter," I chuckled.

"Speaking of birthright, which one will you choose?" Salem questioned, and I groaned loudly.

"Why do I have to choose one? Why can't it be both?" I sighed.

"Maybe you can convince your parents that not only can you handle the responsibility of being demon queen, but you can also handle the responsibility of being the supreme as well," She replied.

"Do you think I can convince them?" I asked.

"You might, but I think it'll be a little hard considering how you're Now the Alpha King's mate," She replied.

"Oh, God. I don't even want to think about that," I groaned. She chuckled.

"The amount of tension and hate between you two is very comical. Just as comical as your mother running away from your father before you were born," She said.

"Don't compare us to them. My parents have some special, unlike me and him, who never will," I muttered.

"That's only because you won't allow something special to happen," She replied.

"Nor will he," I jerked a thumb in Jayden's direction.

"I can see that you're both very stubborn creatures. I wonder who will break first," She said.

"Not me, that's for sure," I rolled my eyes.

"Care to make a wager on that?" She asked.

"No. I'm not falling for that," I responded.

"Oh, come on. It'll be in your very best interest," She said.

"No. It'll be in your best interest, you cunning cat," I hissed. She chuckled again.

"Alright. You're missing out," She murmured.

"Oh. I'm not," I said. I went on to prepare dinner for the both of us.

"Are you ready for tonight?" Salem asked. I sighed loudly.

"I guess," I mumbled as I rummaged through my things. Tonight was the night of a blood moon, which meant that this was when my powers would increase in strength, and my bloodlust would rise too. This means anyone who gets near me has no chance of survival. Because of this, every year since I was five, I've been locked inside one of my trunks that would expand using magic so that I could lie in it. Salem would use her magic to wrap the box in many silver chains and put a lock on it. She'd even use her magic to create metal hooks on the floor so the chains would hold the box just in case I tried to break out, and I tried every year, but I failed. I forgot to add that my hands were wrapped in thick chains along with my ankles, and I'd have a muzzle wrapped around my face to prevent me from biting myself or the chains in there. It was a little much, but when it came to blood moons, demons were insatiable creatures who'd kill everybody within their path. I wasn't like that, but I still wanted to take the precautionary measure of locking myself away so I wouldn't hurt anybody like I did when I was seventeen. A knock sounded on my door, and I saw Eve standing in my doorway.

"Hey, Lani," She smiled.

"Hey, E," I smiled back. I hadn't seen Eve since the day I moved in because Jayden and his parents had given her and her parents an extensive chore list that led to me not even being able to see Eve. It made me so angry that Jayden would treat his family like this, and I've tried talking to him about it, but he ignores me or insults me before walking away. I gave up after a while because I knew that if I tried again, I would surely kill him.

"You ready?" She asked.

"Yeah," I sighed, "I am."

"Don't worry. Salem and I will be here with you all night," She assured me. I smiled softly. Eve has always stuck by me during this occasion every single year, and she has always been there to wake me up in the morning when it ends. She, other than Salem, has always been the first one whose face I'll see when it's over, and I appreciate her for that.

"Thank you, Eve," I said.

"You're welcome. Now let's head to the basement. It's already three, and the sun doesn't set till five," She informed me. I get up and close the drawer I was looking through.

"Salem, it's time," I said.

"Alright," She stretched a bit on my bed and then hopped down. I grabbed a comfortable and fluffy pillow, a thick and comfortable sleeping bag, and a blanket because it gets cold in that box. We walked downstairs and out of the room, then descended into the basement.

"Make sure that Jayden doesn't come in here," I told her.

"I'll try my best, Lani, but you know how it is," Eve replied.

"Oh yeah. I forgot about that," I sighed.

"But I'll try my hardest to make sure it happens. He may be the Alpha King, but you're his Luna," She remarked. I rolled my eyes.

"Yeah. Whatever," I muttered. She chuckled. When we got there, I saw that my trunk had expanded and noticed a comforter and blankets.

"I guess I didn't need this," I giggled. I folded the sleeping bag and placed it on top of a shelf in the corner. I put my pillow inside the expanded trunk and then got in.

"Wow. This is comfortable," I said.

"Thanks. Even if you are going to be a bloodthirsty creature, you still need to be comfortable, especially when you're trying to escape the box and murder everyone," Eve explained. I chuckled at her explanation.

"That is true," I agreed as I handed her my blanket.

"Now come on. Get in," Eve said.

"I'm getting in," I waved her off. I got inside the box and laid my head on my pillow.

"Ahh! So comfy," I sighed in contentment.

"Hold on. Sit up for me, Lani," Eve said. I sit up, and she puts the muzzle on me.

"Now, your mom gave this to me yesterday and some other items we'll be using because she doesn't want you trying to get out of this box at all," Eve informed me. I nodded.

"She told me that this muzzle will be hard for you to get off even when you wake up, so I'll be the one to take it off," She added as she strapped it firmly on. I nodded again.

"You can lay back down now," She said. I laid down and waited for the chains, and Eve returned with the silver chains. I lifted my arms straight up.

"These chains will be hard to break and get off because you'll be weak, and you won't be able to get them off yourself like the muzzle. She also said that you'll be too weak from these chains even to use your witch and demonic powers, which means that you'll be too weak now and in the morning," She said. She wrapped the cuffs around my wrists tightly, and I groaned in pain as they started to burn my flesh. Eve winced and continued wrapping them before putting a lock on them. She lifted both of my legs and did the same process before locking them. She then laid my blanket over me.

"Alright, Lani. I'll see you in the morning," Eve smiled at me. I nodded and smiled back. Slowly the box was closed, and darkness was all I could see. I soon heard the sound of the lock on the trunk click

Okay. Now I'm locked in, so all they have to do is wrap the chains around me and then chain me to the ground.

"Lani, I'll sit down here with you until four-thirty. After that, I got to go upstairs," Eve informed me, "I know that you're probably locked in tight, but your mom told me not to take any chances. The door to the basement, along with any other exits, has been sealed off since yesterday. Your mom did this when she came to visit while you were training. The box also has sealing magic, so you were sealed in as soon as we locked the trunk." Oh wow. My mom never misses a step.

True to her word, Eve kept me company until it four-thirty. I appreciated her for doing that. After she had left, I decided to go to sleep, and I might as well go to bed early because I would be here all night long.

I woke up later that night and knew then that the moon was out for sure. I could feel a vast amount of power surging through me. Due to the increase in strength, I could feel my thirst for blood starting to increase as well. I couldn't control my thirst for blood, and I felt my body begin to transform. I could feel myself becoming less and less like myself. I felt a strong force was holding down my actual self and that a more bloodthirsty version of me was taking over. My body began to move on its own, and I felt the trunk begin to shake. An angry and low growl rumbled in my chest and caused the house to shake.

"Wait! Jayden! Don't go in there!" I heard Eve yell. Jayden. Oh shit.

"Eve! Stand down!" I heard Jayden order in his alpha voice. Eve whimpered. I appreciate her trying to stop him from coming down here and disturbing me.

"I don't think you want to do that," Salem said from the outside.

"And why not?!" Jayden barked.

"She is much more dangerous than you think. Opening that will bring more chaos into this world than you can handle. If you break those chains, she will break free and kill us all," Salem explained.

"I'll kill her before she kills me," I heard him say.

"Your hate for her is clouding your judgment. If you continue to act this way, then you'll make a decision that could potentially kill not just us but the members of your pack as well," Salem explained. He growled in anger.

"Now. I suggest you step away from the trunk and head back upstairs. Don't disturb her until the morning. Even if she is locked in there, a demon is still unpredictable on a night like this, either purebred or not," Salem explained. I growled again and started to thrash in the trunk. I heard Jayden growl again.

"Leave!" Salem demanded. I soon heard the sound of Jayden and Salem leaving the basement.

Chapter Eleven

The morning came, and the box was opened. It had been a long night, but I had made it through. I know the trunk had been damaged. I noticed new scratch marks on the lid. Eve smiled down at me warmly. She took out a key and unlocked the chains. She helped me sit up since I was a little weak. She undid the strap of the muzzle and took it off. I noticed that my wrists and ankles had burn marks around them.

"Come on, Lani," Eve helped me up and out of the trunk. She allowed me to lean on her as she helped me up the stairs. I was fragile the morning after a blood moon, especially since I would be locked in a confined space for a long time and have silver chains to keep me from breaking out. I would be so weak that for three days, I'd get tired quickly from using the slightest bit of magic, so I had to abstain from using it.

"I know you'll probably want to take a bath. Let me go run one for you," Eve told me.

"Thanks, Eve," I weakly said.

"You're welcome," She smiled at me. Eve led me upstairs to my bathroom and sat me down on the toilet while she started a bath. Once Eve filled up the tub halfway, she turned off the spout.

"Okay. Which bath bomb do you want to use?" She asked.

"I'll take the one with rose petals," I replied.

"Excellent choice," She smiled. She grabbed the rose-scented bath bomb from a basket on one of the shelves in the bathroom. She unwrapped it and then dropped it into the bathtub. The bomb fizzled as it started to take effect. Once the water was pink, I began to undress with Eve's help. She helped me get into the tub.

"I'll be waiting outside the bathroom. Okay?" She said, and I nodded as I leaned back against the tub wall. She walked out of the bathroom, and I soon heard her suit against the wall.

After my bath, Eve helped me out of the tub and even helped me get dressed and ready for bed. I thanked her for doing so as she helped me into my bed, and she smiled and tucked me in before I fell asleep completely.

I finally woke up for the day, and I somehow felt different in a way. I felt more powerful and as if more of my powers awoke. These must be the after-effects of the blood moon.

"You woke up quicker than I thought," Salem said.

"What? It's been three days, hasn't it?" I asked.

"No," She shook her head.

"How many days has it been?" I questioned.

"A day," Salem replied.

"A day?! That's impossible. I usually wake up in three days," I said.

"Well, it seems that your time has shortened. Tell me, do you feel any different?" Salem asked.

"Yes," I nodded.

"Then I'd say you've gotten stronger," She smiled.

"So my time has shortened because I've gotten stronger?" I asked. Salem nodded.

"Nice," I grinned.

"As for your friend, she had been called away from here. She apologizes for not being here, but she has a duty to her pack," She said.

"Speaking of her pack, I need to go have a little chat with that mate of mine," I frowned.

"I hope you don't do anything reckless," Salem remarked.

"Don't worry. I won't hurt him too badly," I smirked.

"I guess I'd better come with you," Salem sighed.

"Fine, have it your way," I rolled my eyes.

"Are you sure you want to leave the house in that?" She questioned.

"Salem, I'm going to kick some asses. I'm not going to a fashion show," I replied.

"You still have to look presentable," Salem added. I rolled my eyes and snapped my fingers. I was clad in jeans, a pair of black Nike shoes, and a black t-shirt.

"Happy?" I asked.

"Very. Now let's go," She replied. We both walked out of the house, and the door slammed and locked behind us.

"Let's see how well I can get us to the pack house," I said.

"I'm not ready for this," Salem muttered.

"My teleportation skills are not that bad," I told her.

"Well, when you have to wait for a limb to show up, I'd say it's pretty bad," Salem quipped.

"Maybe this time we won't lose a limb," I said.

"I'd love to see that," She rolled her eyes.

"If you're going to criticize my skills, then I suggest you stay here," I snapped.

"Someone needs to make sure you don't go burning down the place," Salem said. It was my turn to roll my eyes. A flurry of leaves surrounded us, and I closed my eyes. I hope we don't have to wait for a missing limb. When I opened them, we were at the pack house. I looked down, and I sighed in relief—no missing limbs. I looked at Salem, who had no missing limbs either.

"Let's go inside, yeah?" I looked at her, and Salem said nothing as she followed me toward the Black Fang pack house. As we walked inside, all eyes were on us. Many of the pack members growled and bared their teeth at us. One of them tried to swipe at me with their claw-like hand, and I dodged it, and then I continued to Jayden's office. I heard voices coming from the outside. He must be in a meeting.

"Are you going to knock?" Salem asked.

"Nope," I responded. The doors burst open like a large gust of wind had blown through. Quickly, everyone in the room was on their feet, including Jayden.

"What the hell are you doing here?!" He growled. I raised my hand in his direction, and he was thrown back into his chair. The other men in the room roared, but I snapped my fingers. They were now frozen in place. I used another spell to hold Jayden down in the chair. I got on top of the desk and leaned toward him.

"What the fuck?!" He exclaimed. I soon heard footsteps coming down the hallway. The doors slammed shut again, and this time they locked.

"Okay, Jayden. Let's have a chat," I smirked.

"Like hell, I will," He growled. I chuckled.

"If you don't talk with me, then your friends here will stay frozen like that until the next century," I said.

"Fine," He spat, "Talk."

"Great. The first thing I want to say is this, lay the fuck off, Eve. She had nothing to do with the incident where Dad almost killed you, which I hope you did not forget, and the other one before that I cannot seem to recall. Eve and her parents have not a damn thing to do with what I did, so don't punish them for it. If your pack does not stop shunning them, hurting them, or punishing them, I will see that every one of you drops dead instantly one day. The only survivors will be Eve and her family. Eve is my best friend, and I'm getting tired of seeing her come to my house with bruises or cuts," I calmly stated.

"Anyone associated with you is guilty," He growled.

"Eve didn't do anything and never had anything to do with those two situations. You can spout that bullshit about how her association with me is grounds for punishment, but you and I both know what you're doing is wrong, especially considering how she's family," I glared at him.

"I don't care if she is family. I'm not doing anything you say," He snarled.

"Well, well, well," I smirked, "It seems we have to do it one or two ways."

"Two ways?" He looked at me in confusion.

"Yes. The easy way and the hard way," I smiled.

"What's the easy way?" He asked.

"The easy way involves you telling your pack to leave Eve and her family alone without me hurting you," I replied.

"And the hard way?" He questioned. I unfroze one of the guys in the room. I snapped my fingers, and an invisible force bound his arms and legs. The man started struggling.

"The hard way is that I'll kill this gentleman right here before your very eyes without any remorse whatsoever, and I'll even burn down this packhouse while saving Eve and her family," I explained, "Hell, I might even keep you alive and have you watch it."

"Don't agree to it!" The guy said as he struggled more.

"Silence," I hissed. The man went mute behind me. I turned back to Jayden, who was looking at the guy worriedly. He sighed and looked at me with a scowl.

"Fine," He clenched his teeth. I smiled wickedly and gave out a low, maniacal laugh.

"Good, boy," I patted him on his head, and he growled at me inhumanely. I hopped off the desk and headed towards the door.

"Release them!" He yelled.

"I'll release them as soon as I leave this house completely," I informed him. As soon as I reached the door, I opened it slightly and looked at him over my shoulder with a smirk.

"Oh yeah. My parents wanted us to get along, so my mother planned this entire date thing for us tomorrow. We both have to attend, or else she'll skin us both alive," I explained.

"I'll attend no such thing," He bellowed.

"Oh, but you will, or else she'll send my father," I smirked. He growled.

"What time is the cursed thing?" He asked.

"Seven o'clock sharp," I replied, "So clear your Saturday night schedule." With that, I left with Salem, who was close at my heels.

"You still up for that bet?" Salem asked. I laughed.

~*~

"This is torture," I mumbled. My mother was doing my hair tonight for my date with Jayden, which was going to be here in the Black Fang Pack's Territory. The only reason it was going to be here was that Jayden's parents did not trust my parents or me, and I honestly didn't give a shit about their opinions because I disliked them, to be honest.

"How is torture?" Mom asked.

"Because you're forcing two people who hate each other's guys to go on a 'date,'" I responded.

"It wouldn't be so 'tortuous' if you two got along," She hissed.

"Ow!" I yelped as she pulled extra hard on my hair.

"Sorry, honey," She smiled sheepishly. I mentally rolled my eyes.

"This was the only other way I could get you two to communicate. From what I've seen through the crystal ball, you two didn't even communicate, and you both avoid each other altogether," She explained.

"What do you expect? We hate each other," I said.

"And that's unnatural," She replied, "Mates are supposed to carry at least a little bit of love for each other instead of hate."

"Well, not these two mates," I muttered.

"I heard that," She remarked.

"Besides, what's the point of me getting all dolled up for a man I hate?" I questioned.

"The point is that you need to put at least a hundred percent into this thing, even though you do not agree with this idea," She responded.

"The only person putting a hundred percent into this is you," I mumbled.

"I'm only putting in a hundred percent because you're not doing it," She hissed.

"Well, sometimes if someone is not putting in a hundred percent, then the other person would just drop it," I quipped.

"And maybe if some people keep talking like that, then the other person will turn them into a frog and make them live like that for a month," She countered. I frowned and looked away.

"I'm almost done with your hair, sweetheart," She said. I said nothing as she continued to style my hair. I didn't want to go on this 'date,' but after being threatened of never being able to go with Nyra, my mother, or my father on political trips across the world, I caved.

"Alright. Done," Mom announced. I looked in the mirror at my hair, which was now braided half up and half down, style. My makeup was already done, and it consisted of rose gold eyeshadow with black winged eyeliner, a light pink highlighter, and dusty pink liquid lipstick that was smear-proof.

"Alright. Now let's get you out of this robe," Mom said. I stood up from the cute furry chair I was sitting in, and my mom helped me out of the robe, and she laid the robe over her arm.

"Don't you look beautiful," She gushed. I sighed, rolling my eyes.

"Explain to me why this dress is short," I said.

"This is to speed up you and Jayden's journey to your new relationship," She replied.

"What?" I asked.

"Okay. Maybe that was confusing," She muttered.

"You think," I remarked.

"This dress is short because when he and his wolf see you like that, he'll be worshipping the ground you walk on," She informed me.

"Oh, this dress is short because you want the man to rip it off me at first sight? Am I hitting the nail over the head?" I asked.

"Yes, you are, but he can't rip it," She replied.

"Why not?" I questioned.

"That dress is over a thousand dollars," She stated.

"What?!" I practically yelled.

"Calm down. You may think it looks cheap, but the price is nothing to sneeze at," She replied.

"I can calm down when I have a thousand-dollar dress on me," I cried out.

"You can, and you will, or else," She threatened. I calmed down a little as she said.

"So, all we have to do is-" The doorbell suddenly rang.

"Right on time," She smiled.

"Great," I grumbled sarcastically.

"I can't wait for you two to see what I had planned," Mother gushed. I rolled my eyes as I followed her to the door. She turned around.

"Oh no. You wait for my signal, young lady," she said.

"Mom," I whined.

"Uh-uh, young lady. Wait here," She shook her head. I groaned loudly, and she walked downstairs. I soon heard the front door opening and my mother cheerfully greeting him. I heard Jayden tell her that the flowers he had brought were for me, and she told him to hold on to them.

"Amora, Jayden is here," she said. Can I just be struck down right here and now? I took in a deep breath and walked towards the stairs. I slowly walked down because I was not breaking my ankle in these damn shoes. Jayden and my mom, who had a very broad grin on her face, watched me. I had to admit that Jayden looked good in the black Armani suit that he was wearing. Jayden looked at me in....awe? Weird. Jayden soon masked his expression with a blank one. I stood two feet away from him until my mom gestured for me to move closer. I suppressed a groan and moved closer.

"These are for you," he said.

"Thanks," I replied. Mom took them from me.

"You two go have fun," she said.

"I'll try," I mumbled. She shot me a warning look, and I said nothing else. Jayden and I walked outside my house together, and suddenly the cobblestone path leading to my mother's house lit up. I rolled my eyes. Jayden walked down the stairs first, turned to me, and held his hand.

"What are you doing?" I asked.

"Being a gentleman or whatever," He replied.

"Why?" I questioned.

"Because it's our first date," He replied.

"No. I meant, why the hell are you doing this? Because you sure weren't a gentleman when we first met," I said.

"Fine. Your dad visited me earlier saying that if I weren't a gentleman tonight, like holding doors and all that good stuff, he would drag me to Nazareth by my ankles then chop off my balls," He informed. I smirked. I giggled.

"Oh wow," I said.

"Now that we've got that out of the way, can you just take my hand?" He replied. I gently placed my hand in his, and he held it as I walked down the stairs. He let go of my hand and smoothed out his suit.

"Let's get this over with," He muttered. We both began our silent journey down the path toward the woods.

When we reached our destination, I saw a big wooden pergola with vines, a chandelier hanging from the top, and lateens at each top corner. Below it was a small wooden round table for two with a tablecloth on top, wooden chairs, two glass lamps, and gorgeous place settings for two people with expensive dinnerware. Jayden and I walked over toward it. I walked towards one of the chairs, and Jayden walked behind me. He pulled out my chair for me, and I sat down. He pushed it in for me. I thanked him, and he took his seat across from me. Suddenly, a rabbit dressed in a white shirt, a black vest, and slacks appeared before us, and Jayden began growling at him.

"Don't growl. He's not going to harm us," I assured him. He stopped growling and looked at the rabbit warily.

"Good evening, sir and madam. I am Pierre, and I will be your waiter tonight," He said.

"Wow. My mom pulled out all the stops," I giggled. Jayden looked at me oddly. Two menus suddenly appeared before us, and I picked mine up.

"Here's our finest wine selection for tonight, Cabernet Sauvignon," The rabbit poured the wine into the two glasses on the table, "I'll give you both some time to look over the menu." The rabbit left us.

"I guess this is normal for you," Jayden said.

"It is," I replied as I scanned the menu, "My Mom did this for my birthday when I was fifteen, and I was obsessed with Alice in Wonderland. She and my dad wanted to give me the party I desired no matter what, so my mom created a dimension just for me that was like the books and allowed me to live out my Alice in Wonderland fantasy to my heart's desire. I think the dimension is still there because I had begged my mom to let me keep it so my children someday can experience something like it."

"I remember Eve going to some type of party when she was fifteen," He told me. I smiled.

"Yeah. Eve accompanied me that day. We were both in attire that fit the time in which Alice in Wonderland was based," I added, "We both had fun having tea with the Hatter, battling the Red Queen, and painting roses red." He chuckled. I looked at him in suspense. He never showed any joy around me. I went back to looking at my menu, and he picked up his. Soon Pierre came back, and we ordered our food.

The rest of our night was filled with us talking, eating, and, to my surprise, joking around with each. I had to admit that I was wrong about him being a complete and utter brute. He was pretty sweet, and I never thought I'd hear those words come out of my mouth.

We walked back to our house together after dinner and walked side by side toward the house.

"Never did I think I'd enjoy this date with you, the woman who tried to kill me," He said.

"I could say the same for you, too," I murmured.

"For what it's worth, I apologize," He told me.

"I'm sorry too. I get my temper from my father," I replied.

"Same," He chuckled.

"If you want, and it's fine if you don't want to, maybe we can...oh, I don't know, start over and get to know each other," I suggested.

"Do I have a choice?" He joked.

"Now that I think about it, no. No, you do not," I giggled. He sighed loudly, and I laughed again.

"Then, I guess," He rolled his eyes with a smile.

"I will say this, though," I told him.

"What?" He asked.

"You're lucky my grandfather didn't do anything," I responded.

"Why?" He asked.

"Let's just say that he didn't get his nickname, Muerte Negra, for nothing," I giggled as I walked away.

“What does that mean?” Jayden called after me, and I looked at him over my shoulder with a smirk.

Chapter Twelve

"Alan, where have you been for the past few months?" I asked.

"If you're going to tell me some sappy shit like 'you missed me,' then I don't want to hear it," he rudely snapped.

"Bastard," I muttered under my breath. Suddenly, I was thrown back into a tree. Pain shot up my back, and I groaned. I hit the ground with a hard thud.

"Anything else you'd like to say?" He asked with a smirk. I slowly got up as the pain from being thrown into a tree resonated in my back.

"Yeah. Fuck you," I spat. A loud 'swish' noise, followed by my screams of pain, caused me to fall to my knees. Blood gushed everywhere onto the forest floor and the trees. The bastard had cut off my arm.

"If you're going to insult me, then at least make sure you know how to defend yourself. That was way too damn easy for me to do," He hissed venomously. I solidified my blood and was glad at him.

"Now, let's see if you can dodge my next attack," He said. Suddenly he disappeared from his spot, and I looked around the forest for some indication that he was going to strike. I went into a defensive position and closed my eyes. I listened for the slightest movement in the trees, the leaves, or the wind to see where he would strike from.

My eyes snapped open, and I dodged his hand quickly. I used my remaining arm to block his next attack that was going for my stomach. I continued stopping his hits and looking for openings at the same time. Finally, I found an opening, and I took it. I blasted him with my magic straight through the right side of his face.

"Good job," He said and smirked, "Now it's my turn again." His face suddenly grew back to normal. That only took ten seconds. Alan sank into the ground as if he was on an elevator. I watched the ground warily for him as I stood there.

As I stood there waiting for his attack, my other arm was cut off this time, and I cried out in pain and sank to my knees.

"Son of a bitch!" I yelled. My blood sprayed everywhere until I solidified my blood again. Alan appeared before me again; I kicked him in the face this time. I concentrated my powers on my foot and blasted half of his off again on the left side. Half of his brain was now gone.

"Now that caught me off guard," He remarked, chuckling darkly.

"And so did this," I snarled. He laughed.

"You'll get over it," He said.

"How the hell am I supposed to take those home?" I snapped.

"Whew! Look at this mess," I heard Nyra say from behind us.

"Thank God," I mumbled. Nyra walked over and picked up my arms.

"That's enough training for the day," Alan said.

"Day? It's fucking six in the morning!" I cried, "And we had been out here since five am yesterday."

"Well, your training is going to start at five am tomorrow," He said. I groaned loudly.

"Fine," I spat. Alan chuckled and then disappeared.

"I wondered if he was working you to the bone," She said.

"He was, and I'm exhausted," I told her.

"Well, lucky for you, I brought some help," Nyra said. Jayden walked through the forest in shorts with no shoes or shirts on as if on cue.

"What the fuck happened?" Jayden asked, rushing towards me.

"Training," Nyra and I responded in unison.

"Training? What the hell kind of training rips off your arms?" He snapped.

"Demons have intense training from other supernatural," I responded, "It's normal to have your limbs ripped off."

"I don't think I like this type of training," Jayden frowned.

"Well, this training helps her not to get killed so easily," Nyra told him.

"And ripping off limbs is part of it?" He asked.

"Yes," We both responded.

"Anyways. She's going to need help going home, and she can't exactly walk all that well," Nyra informed him.

"I can-" Suddenly, I was tripped. Jayden instantly reached out and wrapped his arms around my waist.

"See? She's falling all over the place," Nyra said.

"She's not as sneaky as she thinks," Jayden thought through our mind link.

"No, she is not," I agreed. Jayden and I's mind link had been closed off because of our previous mutual distaste for each other.

"C'mon, you two. Let's head to your Home so I can reattach these limbs," Nyra said. Jayden picked me up bridal style and carried me in his arms.

"So, how long have you done this intense training?" Jayden asked.

"For eight years," I responded.

"Eight years?" He asked.

"Yeah," I nodded.

"How come you look as if you're in high school?" He asked.

"Hm? Oh, demons stop aging after they turn eighteen, and I'm no exception to that," I responded.

"What about witches?" He questioned.

"They stop aging after they turn twenty-one," I replied.

"Wait. Aren't you twenty-one?" He inquired.

"I am, but my demonic powers came before my witch powers, which means that my body quit aging like most demons," I responded.

"Wow," He said. We finally reached the house, and Jayden carried me inside behind Nyra.

"Alright. Bring her to the kitchen," Nyra said.

"Wait. Won't she get blood on the floor?" Jayden asked.

"My arms are torn off, and you're worried about blood being on the floor?" I questioned.

"Yes," He replied.

"Why are you worried when you don't clean the kitchen?!" I snapped.

"Hey. I clean it," Jayden argued.

"When-" Suddenly, my voice was gone as if someone had turned off the switch for it. I looked over at Nyra.

"Will you stop and just come into the kitchen?" She said. Jayden and I saw that the kitchen floor was covered in plastic, along with the table. Jayden walked over to the table and laid me down on it.

"So, how does this work?" Jayden asked Nyra.

"Watch and learn, Kid, because I'm not great at explaining things," Nyra replied.

"Like that's something to be proud of," I muttered aloud after taking her spell off my voice.

"Remember who's the one reattaching limbs," She murmured. I frowned and went silent.

~*~

"I'm bored," I moaned. I was stuck inside the Black Fang pack house all day with Salem because there had been a horrible rogue attack yesterday. Two children were injured, and both were in critical condition. A teenager had their leg ripped off, and a baby and an adult had also been killed. The pack was out for blood, and Jayden was currently out with his beta, delta, and gamma. Because of the rogue attack, I was moved to his old bedroom until they dealt with this problem.

"You could always practice your magic," Salem said.

"I did that earlier, but you were asleep," I responded.

"Well, then, I don't know what to tell you," She murmured.

"That's true, or I could just go somewhere else," I said.

"Are you crazy? There was a rogue attack, and you're thinking about going somewhere?" She asked.

"Yes. I don't like being here around these people. I hate all of them, and all of them hate me," I answered.

"That may be true, but Jayden specifically ordered you to stay here where his pack members will protect you," she said.

"So what? Those muscle heads can't protect me. Only I can protect myself," I told her. I heard growling from outside the doors. I forgot to mention that he placed bodyguards outside of my door to ensure I didn't escape through there, and he even put some outside to ensure I wouldn't go out the window or something.

"I swear you and your father are just alike," She rolled her eyes, "Both of you are just as reckless as you can be." She shook her head.

"I am not reckless," I rolled my eyes.

"Oh really? Then do you care to explain that time you went out night riding on your mother's broom when you were seventeen, and you somehow ended up destroying the house of a Fae?" She questioned.

"First of all, the bitch deserved it anyway, and second, I was just having some fun," I responded.

"See what I mean? Reckless," she said.

"Whatever. I'm leaving because sitting in a house full of people I hate and love to pull pranks on is boring," I muttered.

"So, you're just going to disobey his orders?" She asked.

"Uh duh," I answered.

"You are an idiot," Salem remarked.

"Well, this idiot is not staying here," I said. I stood on Jayden's bed and made a gun out of my fingers, and I shot at the floor, and a portal opened up.

"You coming?" I asked.

"I guess," She sighed. I turned back and landed on a beautiful, soft bed with an oversized, fluffy comforter and black silk sheets. Salem followed soon after and landed on the bed.

"Nice bed, but where is this place?" She asked, looking around. The landscape around us was stunning and very serene. It was nighttime in this world with many stars adorning the skies and shining brightly; the moon was large and full, there were a few shooting stars here and there, the skies were cloudless, and the land seemed vast and endless. Here below the skies, lightning bugs illuminated the night, and beautiful flowers were in full bloom everywhere in a large field that surrounded the bed I was in; a slight and calm breeze filled the air, and the only sound heard was the breeze ruffling the flowers lightly. It was so peaceful that it made me want to fall asleep.

"This is the dimension that I created. I usually use this whenever I can't sleep or want to get away," I explained.

"When did you create this?" She asked.

"About five years ago. Nyra told me that it was part of my training to create a new dimension for myself, and she told me that many witches before have created dimensions where they have escaped to by themselves or with others," I explained.

"Well, this place is beautiful," Salem said.

"Thank you. It took me five years to perfect it," I smiled.

"Well, you did such a wonderful job," She remarked.

"Thank you," I nodded.

"So, how long have you usually stayed here?" She asked.

"A few days to a week," I answered, "But I make sure to tell my parents so they don't go destroying every corner of the world just to look for me." She chuckled.

"Can this world be detected?" She inquired.

"Not by others. No," I shook my head.

"So I guess this is your little sanctuary," She said.

"It is. Beyond that horizon is a sunny side that I'll go to. The sun isn't too close but isn't too far away, the temperature is at seventy-five degrees, and it's always springtime. There are cherry blossoms in full bloom there, beautiful and peaceful animals there, too, like deer and rabbits, and there's a large grassy field I love to just lay in that's so lush, so comfortable, and so plush. As for the insects, there are some bees, but I created them without stingers because I hate those damn things, and I also created butterflies. It's a lovely place that I can take you to if you'd like," I explained.

"I would very much so love that," She smiled.

"Cool, but let's do that later. I'm kind of sleepy from just laying in this bed," I said.

"How did you get this bed here?" She asked.

"Huh? Oh. I bought it five years ago from this Fae I know. She's a cool girl who knows how to make the best beds in the world. I had asked her to make it for me because I needed something to put in here," I answered.

"The design is unique," Salem remarked.

"Thanks. She makes beds based on your personality and what you like. Since she's known me for a long time, it was easy for her to make it. As for the sheets and comforter, I bought the best ones in the world from another Fae that I know, who made them by hand," I explained.

"Wow. You have excellent connections," Salem said.

"I do," I smiled.

"One more question before we go to sleep," She told me.

"Shoot," I replied.

"How is Jayden going to know that we're here?" She asked.

"Hm? Oh. I left a note and told him that if he wants to come in here, he must walk through his closet door," I answered.

"Oh," She nodded.

"Don't worry. Jayden won't get upset, but if he does, I'll handle it," I yawned.

"Oh," She yawned as well.

"Ready for sleep?" I asked.

"I am," She answered. We both lay down and got comfortable before we drifted into a deep sleep.

Chapter Thirteen

Waking hours later, in my dimension, I found that Salem and I were still alone in this place. I could guess that Jayden hadn't read the note and was probably freaking out. I wouldn't put it past him to do that. I yawned, and soon my feet met the great, plush grass below the bed. I snapped my fingers, and a clock appeared, saying it was five in the morning. Usually, I slept longer in this place, but that's just the effect of this dimension. It's so peaceful and serene that you'll feel sleepy when you enter, and once you finally sleep, you'll sleep for hours upon end. I've done it before. I slept for hours on end. I woke up two days after I started and was very well-rested.

The sound of yawning brought me out of my thoughts. I turned to see Salem yawning and stretching.

"What time is it?" She asked.

"Five in the morning," I answered.

"What the heck? How did we sleep until five in the morning?" She questioned.

"This place makes you feel a sense of sleepiness as soon as you step through, and when you finally fall asleep, you end up sleeping for hours. I've slept for a straight week in here, and I would've slept for a whole month, but my mom had to come to get me," I answered.

"So, there is something in the air, as I suspected," She said as she looked around.

"Yep," I nodded, "And if you don't want to sleep any longer, then let's head back to our world."

"Alright," She nodded and hopped off the bed, and I made the clock disappear.

"How do we get home from this place?" She asked. I snapped my fingers, and a door appeared, and it slowly opened, revealing Jayden's bedroom.

"Like that," I answered. Salem and I walked through the door together, disappearing once it closed. I walked towards Jayden's old bathroom and slipped off my clothes along the way. When I got inside, I started the shower and then stepped in. After my shower, I dressed in jeans, a t-shirt, and sneakers. While Salem and I were sleeping, Alan had sent a message that woke us up for a split second, saying that training was today at seven in the morning. It was already 6:30, so now I needed to be out of the house.

"Salem, stay here and inform Jayden about where I'm going and not wait," I murmured.

"Okay," she said. Smoke began to appear at my feet, and soon I sank into the floor until I completely turned into a smoky shadow. Soon, I was darting out of the house and off pack grounds to my usual spot where I trained. When I finally arrived, Alan walked out of the shadows like a stereotypical movie villain with a cloaked figure behind him.

"What's going on and why?" I cocked an eyebrow.

"Today, we are going to be training," he said.

"No-" A slicing noise was all that was heard before my throat was cut. A scowl made its way onto my face as my wound began to heal, which meant that I couldn't speak for almost an entire day until it healed completely. A cut to the throat was the worst wound to deal with and a pain in the ass.

"Like I was saying, we are going to be training today, but I brought a friend," He informed.

"The one in the stupid cloak?" I mind-linked. The person beside him growled. Well, it's your fault for wearing a stupid cloak. I didn't know it was 'Dress Up Like You're in Some Weird Cult Day.' I would've dusted off my old cape from Halloween when I was seven, and don't ask why I still have it.

"Yes. The one in the stupid cloak is going to help you train," He answered as the person stepped forward.

"What are they going to do? Call on their cult buddies and perform some stupid ritual that won't work. "I asked. Alan chuckled, and the person growled again.

"You have to admit that it's funny," He smirked, "She's got me, of all people laughing." The person huffed in annoyance before finally taking off the cloak.

"Oh wow. The woman takes off the cloak only to reveal how ugly she is," I mind-linked both Alan and the person.

"If I'm just going to be insulted all day, then I might leave," The woman said.

"Leaving won't help. Amora will keep insulting you," Alan told her.

"She needs to respect her elders," The woman hissed.

"I'll respect my elders when they don't look like a gremlin, and a goblin had a love child much more deformed than they are," I shot her. Alan laughed again.

"Alan!" The woman cried out.

"It seems that I can't help you, my dear, because of certain circumstances," He replied.

"And what kind of circumstance would that be?" She spat.

"I'd kill this kid if she insulted me," He deadpanned.

"He's right, and he really would kill me without mercy," I informed the woman.

"And does her father know about that?" She inquired.

"He knows, and he's quite alright with it because her mother will just bring her back to life," He answered.

"And then kill him," I added. "Anyways. We're off-" Suddenly, I was attacked. My leg was suddenly ripped off at where my hip met. Blood spurted everywhere, and I ended up on the ground with a hard thud. I stopped the blood flow and growled at the woman who had my leg in her hand with a smug look.

"Bitch," I growled. The sound of bones crackling caused me to look to see that my leg had grown back.

"That's new," I thought to myself.

"Very new," Alan agreed. I jumped to my feet, a malicious look came over my features, and my eyes met the woman's gaze.

"This is about to get fun," I smirked.

~*~

It was one in the morning, and Eve and I were in the kitchen together. I showed her my new ability in the most unconventional ways. "C'mon, Eve. Just do it," I encouraged. She held the butcher's knife close to her chest and shook her head vigorously.

"Mm-mm," She said, "I'm not doing it." For the past hour or two, while the pack slept, Eve and I were in the kitchen with me, trying to get Eve to cut off my arm.

She was very much against it because she was scared that my arm wouldn't grow back fast enough or that I was pranking her like I sometimes do.

"Eve, I won't hold anything against you if you do it. So do it," I persisted.

"No way, Lani. I'm not doing it," She shook her head again.

"Fine," I wrenched the knife from her hand and raised it above my head. Eve screwed her eyes shut tightly and a smirk formed on my face. The blade was brought down with a loud, evident slicing noise filling the air. I cried loudly at the painful feeling of my arm being sliced clean off. Eve opened her eyes and screamed. To fuck with her, I prolonged the regeneration process and screamed.

"AAAAAAHHHHH! Oh my God! OH MY FUCKING GOD! MY ARM!" I screamed hysterically.

"I knew I should've never let you do this!" She cried.

"This is all your fault!" I screamed as I sobbed. Soon, the sound of footsteps was heard coming down the stairs.

"What happened?" Maybe I can keep up with this facade a little longer since Jayden is here.

"Sh-Sh-Sh-She c-c-c-cut o-o-o-off h-h-h-her a-a-a-arm," Eve sobbed. Jayden looked between us and saw the knife on the counter.

"Why the hell did you allow her to do that?! Are you two fucking crazies?! You're both so irresponsible and reckless!" Jayden yelled. One of the pack members quickly grabbed a towel and wrapped my bleeding arm. It took everything in me not to laugh and to keep a straight face.

"I-I-I-I tr-tr-tried t-t-to t-t-tell h-her.... b-b-but sh-sh-she d-d-didn't l-l-listen," Eve cried. Her mom walked over and hugged her.

"You two should've been more careful," Her Mom scolded, "You two could've seriously harmed yourselves."

"Take her to the hospital wing so we can reattach this," Jayden instructed one of the members. They nodded and started to lead me away. As w were walking, my almost authentic-sounding sobs turned into laughter. The pack member looked at me in confusion, and Eve joined in on the hysterical laughter with me. Using my other hand, I took the cloth from my arm and revealed my arm that started to grow back. Everyone watched in surprise as my arm grew back entirely.

"Eve and I concocted this little joke," I smirked.

"Correction. Amora concocted this plan, and I just went along with it," She spoke up.

"What the? Why the hell would you do that?!" Jayden snapped.

"Just to be funny," I responded, "Plus, I've been bored inside this house since you banned me from training with Alan out in the woods."

"So you did this to get back at me?" He asked as the pack members filed out of the kitchen.

"Yes," I nodded.

"That is so damn childish! I only did it to protect you," He hissed.

"You're not protecting me, dummy," I snapped, "To protect me, you have to allow me to train with Alan so that I won't be such an easy target."

"Who's to say you won't be attacked while training?" He asked.

"You're an idiot. Alan will be there with me, and so will Nyra. They can both help to protect me," I answered.

"And what if they're overpowered?" He snapped.

"Then I'll handle it as best as possible," I responded.

"You're not listening to me," He sighed in frustration.

"If you're not going to listen to me, then I'm going home," I hissed.

"Oh no, you're not," He firmly stated.

"Who's going to stop me?" I snapped.

"Me," He frowned.

"How cute," I sneered as I turned to Eve. "You coming?" I inquired.

"Sure," She nodded.

"I forbid you both from leaving," Jayden snapped. Looking him straight in the eye, I opened a portal and grabbed Eve. She followed me into the portal, and I quickly closed it.

"When you meant Home, I thought you meant your mother's house," She remarked.

"That would've been too damn easy," I shook my head.

"So, how long are we staying here?" She asked.

"I don't know. A week," I answered.

"That's a month our time," She said.

"And?" As Eve followed, I walked towards my dad's palace doors without knocking.

"You asshole! Why do you leave?!" Sale cursed form behind us.

"Damn. I forgot she was at the house as well," Eve remarked.

"Me too," I murmured. We both laughed and continued.

"ABUELITA! It's me!" I yelled out.

"Running to your dad and grandparents after every disagreement isn't going to help," Eve said.

"It is helping," I responded, "It's helping me take time away not to kill him. I don't want to end up like my aunt Theresa on my dad's side. She ended up murdering her mate after a huge disagreement about whether or not pampers or buggies were best." Eve's expression turned blank.

"Is anyone in your family who isn't completely and utterly insane?" She inquired. Silence filled the air between us as I began to think about it.

"Considering how she has to think about it, no," Salem spoke up.

"You already know how my backstory. My mom's sister tried to kill me, my dad's brother tried to kill me because I disturbed his sleep, Alan almost killed me when I was five days old after I had to spit up on his clothes, and I was almost sucked dry by a vampire," I explained.

"You lead a perilous childhood," Eve mumbled.

"It comes with being a rare half-witch, half-demon hybrid that has prophesies written about how she'll destroy the world someday and bring terror and chaos upon those who survive that tragedy," I responded.

"Again, your childhood was much more dangerous than mine," Eve added.

"So was yours by association. Remember the time we almost were torn to shreds by those lycans?" I asked.

"Don't remind me," Eve groaned, "I had nightmares for months after watching your dad tear them to shreds before our eyes."

"Well, he isn't the demon king for nothing," I murmured.

"Whatever," Eve muttered. Ever, Salem and I searched every inch of the palace together and separately, but we couldn't find anyone to no avail.

"Hm. I guess nobody's here," I remarked.

"So what do we do now?" Eve inquired.

"Raid the fridge!" I grinned, "My grandmother always cooks enough for me whenever she, my dad, and grandfather have dinner, just in case I ever feel like dropping by. That's with or without you or Salem."

"I do miss your grandmother's cooking," Eve replied.

"That's the spirit! Now let's go!" I exclaimed.

Chapter Fourteen

"It's been three weeks since we arrived here and three months since we left there," Eve murmured. We were currently sitting on the couch in the lounge room of the palace in Nazareth with comfortable pajamas on our bodies, blankets covering our lower halves, and lots of unhealthy snacks surrounding us. I had placed a large, bright television here so we could watch Netflix and closed black curtains to keep the light from the burning fires of chaos from interrupting our fun.

"Really? My perception of time is off right now," I responded with a mouth full of cookies. It was the truth. I didn't want to keep track of time at all here because it meant that the fun would come to an end.

"This means that I'm the only one who's been keeping track of time," She remarked.

"Pretty much," I mumbled through my stuffed mouth.

"Can you pick if you're going to eat or talk!" She scolded.

"Sorry," I apologized in a muffled voice.

"Madre quit feeding them! As much as I love them both, they're like rats right now. They won't go away if you keep feeding them, especially your granddaughter, who loves using me to run away," My dad said from outside. The doors to the living room burst open, causing light to pour in. Eve and I hissed as we hid under the covers.

"See? They're practically hissing from the slightest bit of light coming into this room," My dad told her. He walked over to the window and quickly shoved open the curtains.

"No! Not the light!" I exclaimed.

"Niños dramáticos culo," My father muttered.

"Bien. Dejaré de alimentarlos," Abuelita sighed, "Y no llame an estas ratas bebés preciosos de nuevo."

"Abuela tiene razón. No nos llames ratas," I spoke up from the blanket. My dad walked over and ripped it away before flicking my forehead hard. He was about to do it to Eve, but he was smacked upside the head.

"Ow!" He yelped.

"¡ Deja de golpear an esas chicas, Valrick, o si no, te pego!" She snapped.

"¡ Acabas de hacerlo!" He exclaimed. She hit him again, and I snickered. My dad glared at the floor as he rubbed the back of his head.

"You two! Clean up this mess, and I mean with your hands and shower. You're going home today," My dad informed me.

"Why?" Eve and I groaned.

"It's been three months in your world, and you two have been lounging around like it's nothing. Salem already went back like a month ago your time, and you two have been just laying around all day and night," He told us.

"It's nighttime?" Eve looked outside in confusion.

"Yes! Can't you tell?" Dad inquired.

"Not really," She answered.

"That's not the point, and the point is that you two need to go home instead of just lounging around my palace like a couple of bums. You both have obligations you need to attend to," He said.

"Do we have to?" Eve and I asked.

"¿Quién demonios creó an estos niños perezosos?" My dad muttered to himself.

"Tú me creaste," I responded smartly. He looked over at me with a glare that had me cringing away as if he had struck me.

"¿Te estás haciendo el listo conmigo? ¿Tengo que llamar a tu madre?" He threatened.

"No, señor," I mumbled, looking down.

"Eso es lo que pensé. Ahora Levántate y haz lo que te pregunté o si no," He ordered. My father and abuelita left the room so Eve and I could start. It took us almost an hour to clean up this place, but we did it. Afterward, we showered and got dressed before packing our bags to leave.

"You two, Amora especially, need to stop running to Bronwyn or me every time there's a problem. Don't act like you don't do it either, Eve," He told us, "You both need to face them head-on like adults. We, your parents, aren't always there when you guys want to run away from your problems. Amora, go talk it out with Jayden about this whole safety thing. As much as I want you to reject that bastard and rip out his throat like the heartless creature you were born to be, you can't because that's your true mate, and you two can't keep butting heads every single time, no matter how much I enjoy it."

"You were right. Your family is insane," Eve whispered to me.

"Yep," I whispered back.

"Just talk it out with him, and don't get too angry, Amora," he said.

"Fine," I mumbled.

"And if you feel like rejecting him, then ripping out his throat and burning down the entire pack house with only Eve and her parents as the only survivors, then I'll be fine with it," He added.

"What is with you and ripping out throats?" I asked.

"Your mother and I haven't had sex in a while, so I'm a little frustrated," He responded.

"OH MY GOD! DAD!" I yelled.

"What? Blame your mother," he said.

"I think I'm gonna throw up," Eve muttered.

"BYE, DAD!" I exclaimed. I opened a portal, and Eve and I stepped through it.

"Love you, honey!" He spoke.

"Love you too, Dad," I muttered. The portal closed, and I gagged loudly.

"That was so disgusting," I said.

"You're telling me. That was worse than that curse placed on us by that voodoo lady," She added.

"I almost forgot about that," I murmured.

"How could you 'almost forget' when she made it hard for us to walk in the sun without our skin burning?" She asked.

"It was taken away as quickly as possible," I replied.

"Two weeks isn't quick," Eve glared at me, "Plus, I still get itchy if I'm in the sun too long."

"Seriously?" I asked.

"Seriously," She responded.

"You better tell my mom because she's the one who took it off," I said.

"I will," She responded.

"You know, after my mom took the curse off, my dad ripped the woman apart and had my abuelita cook her alive. Her, my grandfather, and dad ate her," I informed, "Plus, I got a little nibble on the side of her heart. Okay. Maybe a big nibble." Eve looked at me in shock.

"You were born a monster," She whispered.

"Oh please," I scoffed, "Don't act like you didn't see me ripping out the throat of some evil Fae and eating their organs back when we were kids."

"I almost forgot about that until you brought it up," Eve hissed.

"Whoops," I giggled. She rolled her eyes with a grimace.

"Any more horrifying things you want to share with me?" She asked.

"I killed a shapeshifter last month that had been raping women and molesting children, then I ate its heart and brain," I murmured.

"You are a demon," She whispered.

"Half-demon," I amended.

"Correcting me on your race should be the least of your worries, considering how my perception of you right now is that you're evil," Eve told me.

"What do you expect from someone who is practically born evil? You expect them to be all rainbows and sunshine?" I inquired.

"YES!" She exclaimed.

"Too bad. You're stuck with my evil self until the day you die," I said.

"Oh, moon goddess!" She groaned.

"The moon goddess hates demons, to be honest," I murmured.

"Of course, she does. Your ancestors caused a lot of death, destruction, and chaos," She answered, "It doesn't matter to me if she punished me for being friends with you because you're not like them. You're good, even though you kill people and eat their hearts like some weirdo."

"The heart is the most delicious part of the body and right next to the brain and the soul," I said.

"Do I even want to know about the soul thing?" She asked.

"Nah. You shouldn't," I shook my head.

"Good."

~*~

I walked home from yet another long night of training only to find the pack house under attack by some rogues. Great. This is just what I needed. A fucking rogue attack is happening while I'm on my way home, practically exhausted from a seventy-two-house training session with Alan. From what I could see, Jayden and the other male and female members were fighting against them and getting the shit beat out of them. A few members' bodies were lying around with their throats ripped out and blank stares frozen on their faces as their blood stained their skin and the ground. I'd better help them and feed off the chaos around me.

"They could use it," I murmured as a rogue tried to attack from behind me. My body transformed, and my demonic form took over, and this time I had a tail that I hated with a passion. Quickly, I turned and faced the fucker with a malicious, ear-splitting grin on my face. The rogue growled and lunged at me, but I caught it by the throat with my hand. My grip on its throat became so painful that it whimpered and struggled against me until a loud snap was finally heard. The filthy mutt went limp, and I dropped it to the ground before turning into a dark shadow on the floor. I appeared in front of Jayden's beta, Jake, who was struggling with a rogue trying to rip out his throat. I picked up the filthy creature by its jaw. I grabbed its snout and ripped it in half. Jake looked on in horror as I did it. I would use my magic, but I'm a little too bloodthirsty and chaos thirsty at the moment to even do that. Ripping them apart is the only way to satisfy the two for the moment.

"Aren't you going to help?" I asked. He snapped out of his horrified daze and scrambled away quickly. Another growl caused me to look forward to finding a rogue bigger than the others in front of me.

"Let me guess. You're the leader of this rag-tag group?" I smirked. He growled and stalked out of the shadows.

"I must be right then," I chuckled softly, "It makes sense that you're the leader because you all look the same." He circled me with his wild eyes trained on me. I knew he was waiting for the perfect time to strike, and I knew he needed me to drop my guard before he did, but that was going to happen as he wanted. Yes, you heard me right. I'll let him get his little licks in before I take action. The only conflict I had now was between ripping out his rib cage or leaving him alive and taking him with me to my dad's home. Hence, a couple of ravenous demons my grandfather had in his pit would tear him limb from limb as I watched with one of his little subordinates whose arms and legs would be cut off.

Because I had been brainstorming ideas of how to torture him, I suddenly felt a slight sting from my arm being ripped off. I looked over to see that my arm was a few yards away. Slowly, my head turned, and I looked at him with wild, malicious eyes. He growled and moved out a few feet as soon as he felt the horrible aura surrounding me. The birds in the trees flew away in fear from the horrific emotion they were feeling, and everyone around froze in place. I could feel the fear radiating off of Jayden, his pack members, and the rogues, but I didn't care as long as I could feel the blood of this parasite splattering on my face, running down my arms, and dripping onto my lips.

"My turn," I said. Dark laughter escaped my lips as I sunk into the ground. The leader ran towards me, but I managed to go down before he could catch me. Underground, I knew the rogue was searching for me, and I knew that although he was angry, he was scared. He was scared of the unknown, and I couldn't blame him. I'd be terrified if I had a demon drunk off of the chaos and death around her.

When I finally came up from the ground, I was close behind him while he turned his back, looking for me. I grabbed his tail, and he yelled in surprise.

"Gotcha," I chimed creepily. I dragged him back as he howled and scratched his nails against the ground in fear. He was against me as he was dragged into the sinking ground with me. The others looked on in horror as he went down with me.

Hours later, I emerged from the ground with blood spattered all over me. As he saw me approach, Jayden was leaning against a tree with a grim expression.

"How'd it go?" I inquired.

"We killed them all," He answered.

"That's great. I'll be inside taking a shower," I told him.

"That was terrifying to witness," He said. I paused and turned to look at him.

"So? What's the big deal?" I asked.

"The big deal is that I'm a little wary of you right now," He answered truthfully.

"Why, because I killed a rogue?" I rolled my eyes.

"Not just that," He responded, "It was the look you had as you did it."

"I can admit that I probably looked scarier than I should, but who cares. I'm half demon," I said.

"I care, Amora. Not only did you kill them, but you looked unhinged, and you looked like you would kill just about anyone near you," He argued.

"Jayden, I have a little more control over my actions than you think," I hissed.

"Do you really, Amora? Just last week, you almost killed me for pissing you off, and had Eve not called your mom, then we wouldn't be having this conversation now," He snapped, "Not to mention that you almost killed one of the members for bumping into you. Let's not forget that you snuck into my parents' bedroom one night to try and kill my mother, who merely insulted you." Maybe I didn't have the best self-control when it came to people pissing me off, and perhaps I've been close to killing people, except Eve and her parents, within this pack more than once. They all piss me off each second of the day.

"So what are you trying to say?" I asked.

"I want you to leave," He sternly answered. Silence filled the air between us as I thought about what to say until I finally nodded.

"Okay. I'll leave, Jayden," I responded, "I'll be out by today." I turned into a shadow and farted towards the pack house to pack my things. When I got to the room I shared with Jayden and saw Salem lounging peacefully on the bed.

"Salem, we're leaving," I told her.

"Why?" She asked, looking at me worriedly.

"They're sick of me here," I answered.

"Oh no. What happened?" She groaned.

"I'm unstable, he says," I swiftly replied.

"He's finally gotten tired of you, huh?" Salem said. I nodded as I used my magic to pack up everything in this packhouse of mine.

"Even though we're leaving, I'm going to keep the charms up in this house," I told her.

"That's nice of you," She said. Once my things were packed, and in one of the three trunks I had, I snapped my fingers and sent it to my Nyra's house.

"Come on, Salem. We need to head to the other house," I informed as I walked towards the closet door. I opened it, and it led me through my former bedroom's closet. Salem followed after, and I used my magic once more to pack any and everything I had brought here into the two remaining trunks of mine, and I sent them to Nyra's house.

"Is that everything?" Salem asked.

"Yeah. That's everything," I sighed.

"Are you okay with this, Amora?" She questioned.

"Yeah, I'm fine with it. It was only a matter of time before he finally asked me to leave. I'm happy about this," I chuckled. She said nothing else, and we went through the closet door of this room that led us to my old bedroom in Nyra's home. The door closed, and I sighed to myself. I snapped my fingers repeatedly, and everything returned to its original spot before I left.

"Nyra! I got kicked out!" I yelled.

"Alright! We'll talk once you take a shower!" She responded. I giggled. It felt good to be home.

15

Chapter Fifteen

My mother frowned at me. "You are just like your father and his family. You all don't know how to control yourselves or that anger," My Mom scolded. She had found out through Eve's Mom that I had been asked to leave, and she was very livid once she found out why. She had been scolding me for over an hour about my behavior towards that pack, and I can't say that I don't feel a bit bad because they all had to deal with me, even though half of them were a bunch of bastards, and bitches, pun intended.

"Not to mention that you've almost killed many people within that pack and continued to live there like it wasn't a problem! Do you know how bad this looks within the supernatural community? Do you know how it makes your father, and I look? Do you know that people might think you're unfit to rule over one of our domains? Do you know how many people will be wary even to want to speak to you about diplomatic situations because they fear you will only use violence to solve it?!" She yelled.

"Mom, I'm sorry," I said.

"I'm not the one you should be apologizing to!" She hissed.

"How can I apologize when he won't even allow me within at least fifty feet of the pack house or won't even talk to me?" I inquired.

"Oh, God. How did you find this out?" She asked.

"Eve told me yesterday when she came over. He sent her because he knows I won't even dare to harm her," I answered. She told me this yesterday after I had tried calling him a few days after he kicked me out.

"Of course not. You two have been friends for years," She rolled her eyes.

"Yes, we have, and she comes before him," I murmured.

"And that's another problem I need to bring up," She told me.

"What?" I asked.

"That little attitude of yours towards him," She answered.

"What do you mean by that?" I looked at her in confusion.

"You'd rather save Eve over him, which is very selfish considering how he's your mate," She told me.

"So?" I shrugged.

"So that's the problem. Your relationship with him may have changed, but you don't care about his safety," She shook her head.

"Oh, come on, Mom. I do care about his well-being," I scoffed.

"Do you? Because you've tried to kill him many times without any mercy," She said. She had a point. It didn't seem like I cared about him with how I acted toward him, but I did. I care about him in my special way, even though he pissed me off half the time with his stupidity. There were times when I showed genuine caring for him, like sometimes when he would be in his office sleeping on the couch, I'd use my magic to send his body upstairs to our room, and then I'd tuck him in. When he would forget to eat, I'd send food his way so that he could. If he protested against eating, I'd appear before him and use my magic to hold him down to force him to eat. When he couldn't sleep sometimes, I'd take him to the dimension I created so he could rest on his own and bring him back fully rested for whatever meeting he had to go to. There was a long list of things I did for him that most, including himself, don't know about.

"Mom, it may not seem like it from the outside, but I did care for him. I did a lot of things for him that he doesn't even know about," I responded, "It kind of hurts to hear you say that I didn't care." Her expression softened a little when she heard this.

"Did you?" She asked. I nodded. Suddenly, I felt her probing my mind to detect any hint of a lie, and when she found nothing, she nodded.

"I believe you, sweetie, but I still don't like that 'I will kill everyone, except for my best friend and her parents' attitude. It's the worst thing someone, especially your mate, can hear," She said. I groaned loudly.

"You know it's true, Amora. I hate that so much," She said.

"Well, if his pack members weren't a bunch of assholes, then maybe I'd be much nicer," I told her.

"I swear you're going to be my death," She muttered. I said nothing.

"I have to go now, but you need to try and invite him over to talk," She instructed.

"How? He won't talk to me at all," I replied.

"Well, force him to do it," She said.

"Uh-uh. I'm not going to force someone who doesn't want to do anything they don't want to," I shook my head.

"You are so hypocritical that I can't," She rolled her eyes.

"Am not," I argued.

"Yes, you are. You've forced Eve to talk it out with you more than once when you were arguing, and you've forced your father to talk to me on more than one occasion," She explained.

"Those times involve petty arguments between us where we were both wrong, and you and dad have been arguing for years, so excuse me for getting annoyed," I replied.

"The point still stands that you force people to do things they don't want to," She said. Mentally, I rolled my eyes.

"Fine. I'll get him to talk to me," I grumbled. Snapping my fingers, Jayden suddenly appeared before us naked as the day he was born with water sliding down. The sight made my panties dampen.

"Oh wow. What a big dick," My Mom remarked. Jayden's hands flew to cover it unsuccessfully in embarrassment.

"What is the meaning of this?" He growled.

"My Mom wants us to talk," I answered with my eyes trained on his "friend."

"Well, I don't want to," He stubbornly replied.

"Well, you don't have much choice," I said, finally looking at him.

"I'm leaving," Mom announced, "I'll see you in at least a month or two." I knew she was thinking about going to Nazareth to see my dad just so they could have sex, which was gross to even think about. Jayden moved his hands and headed for the door, and I used my magic to lock it and create a barrier preventing him from leaving.

"Amora, let me out," He growled.

"Uh-uh. Not until we talk," I replied.

"Why? I've said all that needed to be said," He sighed.

"Yeah, well, my mom wants us to talk or whatever," I rolled my eyes, "Plus, even if you leave this room, there's no guarantee that we'll be able to leave this house."

"Did she put a spell on this house?" He frowned.

"Yep," I nodded, "So there's no way we're leaving until we talk.

"Fine, but can you get me some clothes?" He asked.

"No," I nodded, "I like you that. Just naked and ready."

"Ready for what?" He looked at me in confusion, and I smirked at him, and he shook his head with a roll of his eyes.

"We're not going to be doing that, Amora," He said, "You're too unpredictable."

"You're so cautious of me that you wouldn't even consider having sex with me? Are you fucking kidding me?" I asked in disbelief.

"Yes, I'm cautious of that because I don't know if you'll lose control," He responded. This is why he keeps getting almost killed by me, and he says shit like this to piss me off.

"You piss me off," I hissed.

"And there's the problem. You get angry too easily," He remarked.

"Oh fuck off," I snapped.

"Another thing you do. You get angry when people tell you the truth, and you just shut down," He pointed out.

"No, I don't, Jayden," I snarled.

"See? You're even growling at me right now," He replied. I glared hard at him, but I stopped.

"You're unstable, Amora," He said, "You're unstable and dangerous to not only me but the other members of my pack who are not my cousin. I can't have you around them or me because who knows what you might do someday if pushed over the edge."

"So what if I am?" I asked.

"Then that means that I can't be around my mate if she's like this," He answered.

"So, are you saying you want to reject me?" I looked at him.

"If you stayed in the pack house long enough, it would've gotten to that point," He answered.

"I'm not talking about a damn 'what if,' Jayden. I'm talking about now," I snapped. He let out a loud sigh.

"I've considered it," He said. Did it hurt to hear him say that? Yes, it did, but then again, I wouldn't be angry if he did because our whole bond is out of whack.

"So, are you going to do it?" I asked.

"No," He shook his head.

"Then what's the point in keeping me around if you won't talk to me or anything?" I asked.

"I wish I knew myself," He answered.

"You're a fucking idiot, Jayden," I shot at him, "How the hell do you not know why you're keeping me around?" He glared at me.

"Because I don't know, Amora," He clenched his teeth.

"That's not good enough for me," I shot at him.

"That's not good enough for you? That's rich," He laughed humourlessly.

"You're so insufferable," I rolled my eyes.

"So are you, sweetheart, but at least I won't have to see your face every day," He shot at me.

"I'm glad as well because at least I won't have to hear the stupid shit that comes out of your mouth," I spat venomously.

"At least I won't have to deal with some psychotic, obnoxious half-demon who doesn't know how to control her fucking anger and acts like such a goddamn know-it-all!" He retorted.

"Oh fuck off, you stupid mutt," I hissed, "You get on my fucking nerves!"

"Same to you, demon bitch," He bitterly said.

"It's better to be a demon bitch than some unfit king of mongrels that lick their balls," I shot at him.

"This is coming from a spoiled brat who needs mommy and daddy to help her fix her problems," He quipped.

"At least my father isn't mated to some dumb bitch like your mother," I smirked.

"Don't you talk about my mother like that," He snarled, standing up?

"Why? It's true. She's a dumb bitch who doesn't know a damn thing about politics and did nothing but spread her legs before you were even born," I said.

"Don't you talk about my mother like that," He fumed.

"Why? It's true. Your mother was nothing but an" In an instant. He was on me. He wrapped his large hand around my throat and lifted me, so I was at eye level with him.

Chapter Sixteen

"So that limp wasn't there before," Salem said. I shot daggers at her with my eyes, and she just smirked. I continued to shovel Frosted Flakes into my mouth.

"He did a number on your neck," Salem remarked, "So the rumors are true. Male wolves are aggressive." I ignored her and ate my cereal quietly. Salem was right. The skin from my neck to my breasts was covered in hickeys, there were some bite marks here and there, my ass cheeks were both red and bruised, my neck had handprints on it, and I was still sore down there, so I had a limp, and my voice was gone. I would heal it, but he promised to show no mercy if I did, so my dumb ass submitted. I still want to kill him with my bare hands.

"Oh my God. You look like shit," My Mom said as she walked into Nyra's kitchen. Can everyone stop fucking pointing this shit out? It's bad enough that I can barely sit down without hissing, but I didn't need them pointing out how much I look like shit.

"It takes me back," She sighed.

"Don't you start reminiscing your gross memories around me," I mind-linked at my mom.

"Oh, so you lost your voice last night too?" She asked.

"Yes," I grumbled into her mind.

"What did you say that made him do that to you?" She asked.

"I called his mom a whore in front of him, and he got mad," I answered.

"He got mad, and he got rough," Salem teased.

"Oh, shut the hell up!" I snapped. She and my mom howled with laughter at my apparent irritation.

"It's not our fault that you got in trouble with your mate," my mother chortled.

"Oh, leave her alone, you two. She's had enough teasing this morning alone," Nyra said.

"Fine. Fine. We'll stop," Salem chuckled. My mom sat at the table with a cup of coffee in hand.

"So, did he stay the night or leave?" She asked.

"He left," I replied.

"Did you use protection?" She inquired.

"No, and we didn't need it," I responded.

"Why not?" She asked with a frown.

"He made her swallow," Salem spoke up. My cheeks burned in embarrassment as soon as she said that.

"Oh wow. Smart man," My mom chuckled, "I was right about him being a great addition to the family."

"He didn't leave quietly?" Salem smirked. I shook my head.

"I'm glad I was out of the house until now," Nyra said.

"Hopefully, he didn't pull out," My Mom sipped her coffee.

"Well, he did pull out," I muttered in her mind.

"Aww, man," She whined.

"And from what your memories tell me, he took you in the shower twice," Salem informed.

"Wow. Those male wolves, especially alphas, are insatiable," Nyra remarked.

"An alpha king is ten times worse, and they just Good your back out six ways to Sunday," My Mom said.

"Oh, believe I know," Salem sighed dreamily.

"But nothing beats demon kings and their sex drive. That's why Valrick has over thirteen siblings," My Mom replied.

"Can we not say nasty things at the table? Kay? Thanks," I mind-linked all of them.

My throat began to itch a little at the thought of that day when he completely went crazy on me like a rabid dog. The memory of it was still burned into my mind, and I don't think I could ever scrap it out of there if I wanted to.

"Why? It's true, and your mother was nothing but a-" In an instant. He was on me. He wrapped his large hand around my throat and lifted me, so I was at eye level with him.

"Don't you ever talk about my mother like that, you bastard child," He gritted his teeth. I glared back at him could do it at that moment, spit in his face. That made him angry, and that made him so very angry. He threw me on my bed and wiped the spit from his face. I started to get up, but he quickly turned me over to my stomach and held me down using one hand. He yanked down the shorts I was wearing swiftly.

"Let me go!" I growled. His large hand came down hard against his ass and jiggled. I howled in pain.

"Fuck you!" I spat venomously. He sent another hard slap to it, and I screamed. His hits fucking hurt. He continued smacking me on that cheek until it was very red and sore. He gave me the other one the same treatment as tears streamed down my face while I sobbed for him to stop.

When I thought it was over, he tore my underwear to shreds and shoved two digits deep inside me. I grasped loudly at the intrusion and tried to move away, but he pressed my body hard into the mattress. He pumped his fingers in and out of me quickly.

"P-Please.....K-Jayden.....st-stop!" I begged.

"Shut the fuck up and take it, bitch!" He growled as his digits rammed in and out of me. This was a side I had never seen from him before, and it scared me, to be honest because I'd never provoked him to this point. It terrified me because he was being so rough with me, and he completely shattered the attitude I had.

"Look at who's the whore now," He sneered as he fingered me. My only response was a moan as he made me feel like a bitch. He smacked my ass hard, causing me to gasp and moan simultaneously.

"K-Jayden....I-I-I'm.....c-close!" I exclaimed. He yanked his fingers out of me, and I whined until I felt him spit on my pussy. I practically jumped at the feeling of it on me, but that was short-lived by him spreading apart my cheeks and attacking my pearl like a wild animal.

"Oh....fuck...." I moaned out loud. It was so nasty to have him do that, yet it felt so good. It felt so damn good to be treated this way, but I'll never admit this and never admit it to him out loud. He smacked my ass, and I gasped as my hands grasped the sheets hard. He continued to slap it hard as he ate me out. His tongue whipped around my pussy skilfully, driving me crazy. I was grinding and whining my hips to meet his tongue with each stroke he gave me. My juices leaked onto the bed as he got sloppy and nasty, causing my back to arch.

"F-fuck.... Jayden!" I moaned. It was only a matter of time before I would cum. He removed his mouth, and a whine escaped my lips. Two of his digits plunged inside me, and I felt myself cum from that simple action. Wasting no time, he turned me over to my stomach and placed his fingers against my lips. I took them into my mouth and sucked on them slowly and sensually while he watched me with a glare on his face. He positioned his cock near my entrance and pushed in without warning. He gripped my hips harshly and rammed into me.

"Jayden!" I screamed. He rammed into me harshly. My back arched as I became the victim of his savage-like fucking. It was so bad, yet it felt so good just to be treated like this. My more demonic side wanted more of this merciless fucking that I was being subjected to, while my more human-like side wanted to crawl away into a hole like a coward. But fuck it anyway. My momma didn't raise any damn little bitch.

"Fuck....you tight whore," He groaned, gripping my hips with his hands. Unknowingly, his claws had grown out, digging deep into my skin to draw blood. The warm black liquid stained the sheets I was gripping onto for dear life and my skin. His class continued to dig into my skin, which made me even wetter.

His large hand came down upon my round bottom and struck it hard. A large yelp tore from my throat and soon turned into a shameless moan of pleasure from me. He continued to smack my ass repeatedly as he pounded my snatch like it was his worst enemy. The head of his cock continued to greet my womb like an enemy out for blood. I began to feel an orgasm approach.

"Shit. You demon sluts have them. Best. Fucking. Pussy," he said with each thrust. My only response was a cry of pleasure.

"Jayden....I-I'm....I'm... I’m...CLOSE!" I cried out. He grabbed my hair, yanking me back into a painful arch. He leaned down with his lips formed into a malicious sneer near my ear.

"I don't give a fuck, you stupid slut," He harshly whispered into my ear, "I'm oozing to fuck this pussy until you show me some fucking respect, bitch."

He raised and released my hair. Those harsh words sent me over the edge and caused me to climax hard on his cock. He ignored it and kept going as if I hadn't just done that. My essence dripped onto the bed and started to soak the sheets a little. My hands clutched the beds like a lifeline as the man behind me took his anger out on my poor pussy and me.

Using the hand that had grabbed my hair, he lifted my right leg and slanted it over his hip. With this position, he could go deeper and leave me with no room to escape, which was what I was planning to do after hearing what he had to say.

"Who knew that the ruthless demon was so submissive in bed?" Jayden taunted darkly.

"P-Please....K-Jayden!" I cried out.

"You look so good laying there, Amora," he teased ruthlessly. The way he was speaking to me started to make me feel a little embarrassed about the predicament I was in the right. This was my punishment, and I mean reward, for poking the wolf, and I didn't think he would react this way.

"It's fucking sexy seeing the daughter of the most feared demon and taking my cock like the whore she is," He grinned wolfishly. I moaned in response.

"You look like you're enjoying this, Amora," He taunted again, "Are you enjoying this?"

Trying to form the words I wanted to say in response to his question was hard, and it was hard even to concentrate when he was dominating me like this.

"No response, eh?" He smirked. Was this embarrassing? You bet your ass it was, but it was also very arousing. His claws continued to puncture my skin.

"F-Fuck....y-you.... d-damn....ah!" I stuttered. He smacked my ass hard again. I wish he would get enough of doing that, but it doesn't seem like it. One of his hands snakes up my back and grips my hair. One of his claws had scraped my scalp, causing me to hiss in pain. My bare back was against his hard chest. His hand that held my hair was now tightly wrapped around my throat. The oxygen in my lungs became restricted.

Both hands were covering him to try and pry them off before he did anything further, like kill me, for instance. He squeezed my throat, and I felt lightheaded from this action.

"Am I too rough for you, Amora?" He whispered into my ear. His grip became even tighter. Even speaking was hard as I allowed him to do whatever he wanted to my body. His choking me heightened the entire experience for me and, shamefully, made me even wetter.

"Ooh! It seems like the demon princess loves it," He cooed into my ear. His other hand slipped down in front of my body. He pressed his thumb against my bundle of nerves and began to rub it in fast circles. My back arched against his chest, and my hips met his thrust for thrust. This was so bad, and yet it felt so good. Why didn't I piss him off sooner?

Another orgasm, much more potent than before, had come. He squeezed my neck harder and punished my poor pussy as I came on his dick. My body began to shake from how powerful it was, and my knees began to feel weak, making it hard for me to stay on my knees like this. Soon, he came inside of me, much to my chagrin.

He released me, and my body, weak from that orgasm, fell onto the bed as he lazily pumped inside me. The mix of my essence and his leaked out of me and onto the sheets. He turned me over onto my back, and I weakly used my hand to push him away, to no avail. When I looked at him, I didn't see a man. No. I saw a wild animal. His claws were out, his canines were now out, and his eyes were flickering between his wolf's eyes and his human eyes. A gasp made its way from my throat at the sight of him looking more animal than human.

Without warning or even realizing it, he thrusted inside my anus. I cried out in pain from the sudden intrusion and used the strength I had left to try and push him away, but it was to no avail. His hands gripped my thighs and spread them apart as far as they would. His claws had once again dug into his skin. With no regard for how I felt, he began to move.

"Ugh! Fuck, you feel so good," He groaned. The discomfort I had felt was starting to fade away as pleasure took over. I haven't done this in so long, and I felt like a virgin when it came to this sort of thing.

He lifts me with my legs resting on his biceps and fucks me hard and fast. My arms wrapped around his as he ravaged my body like his true animal. He buried his head into my neck and bit down hard. He littered my neck with as many hickeys as he could and even a few bite marks that I knew would be there till the next day. I cried out in pain with a moan following after. My pussy was leaking my essence and his cum onto his cock.

With a roar, he came inside of me again. He pulled out and lowered me so I was bridal-style in his arms.

"Let's go take a shower," He gave me a wolfish grin. An expression of fear came over my features at the sound of that suggestion.

The rest of my morning was filled with jokes about me and my voice, plus the ruthlessness he showed to my body last night. I didn't see how this shit was funny when it looked like he had beat my ass. Because it hurt too much, I went to my room to lie down. My mom, Salem, and Nyra left to do their separate things while I was left home alone. As soon as my body hit my bed, I fell asleep.

When I woke up, my stomach was growling for two reasons, food and chaos. It had been exactly five days since I left, and my hunger, confusion, and destruction had grown considerably. Usually, I could push it back into the far corners of my mind like some weird, tiny craving, but now it was different. It was now added to my diet. How did I get my daily chaos and destruction filled? I disappeared to my dad's place and committed a couple of horrible and heinous acts, then came back fully refreshed so that I didn't go out into the world and cause it. Getting my fill of it slowed my aging process by hours so that I would age very slowly. This takes "Black Don't Crack" to a whole new meaning.

Slowly, I walked out of my room and into the kitchen. I could tell I was still home alone since Nyra wasn't doing her usual bedtime ritual, nor was Salem creeping around here like some thief in the night. Yawning, I scratched my stomach as I went to the vintage fridge Nyra had kept for decades. She claims it's because it's still running the same as it did, even though I know she's using magic to keep it like that, and she loves the nostalgia that comes with it. The fridge was ice and all. It used to be pretty pastel pink, but Nyra turned it black to fit the dark aesthetic of the house, which was understandable. It didn't make the fridge any less cool.

I bent down and saw a week's worth of food in Tupperware bowls. This let me know that Nyra and Salem were going to be away for a while, which meant that I had some freedom around the house. I took out one of the bowls and smelled the contents. It smelled like a very spicy duck soup that would burn off the tongue of any human who tried to eat it. I loved my half-demon heritage; I could eat anything hotter than hell itself without a problem. I closed the fridge and saw a note on top.

Dear Amora,

Since Salem and I will be gone for a while, I left some food in the fridge for a full week. After that, you're on your own, kid. Make sure you clean up after yourself, clean your room, and make your bed, as yada, yada, yada. Also, there's a little booze in our secret cabinet with a little medicine to heal your throat, so drink up! If Morgan calls, tell her to eat toad shit and choke on it. She's been calling me to bother me about the damn summer Solstice festival taking place months from now, and it's getting on my nerves. Man, I wish her old ass would drop dead already. Enough of my ranting, Salem, and I love you. Bye.

Sincerely,

Nyra

P.S. The Fae King and his son will drop by in two days for this potion I made. It's on the top shelf of the potion cabinet, wrapped in a pretty velvet bag. Just hand it to them and get the money. Whatever you do, don't let them charm you. They're sneaky playboy bastards who will do anything to get into your britches.

Amora chuckled at Nyra's note and left it where it was. What she said about the Fae King was true. Those beautiful bastards loved to charm the shit out of you with their honey-like words, and then BAM! You're pregnant with one of their little fuck boy/fuck girl kids who repeat the damn process. The worst the Fae can ever mate in the supernatural world are sirens, those breathing sushi bitches. Once you mix the honey-like words of a Fae with the deadly voice of a siren, you get some annoying ass bastard child who can sing you to death and sweet talk you like no other.

Who would want to even sleep with a siren in the first place? Their mates, but who would honestly say they'd like to sleep with someone who swims, sleeps, eats, and poops in the same water they live in? That's just gross, especially considering how their origin is also disgusting. Do you want to know how those fish fucks came to be? They were once a demon that could sing you to your death and then started fucking mermaids like no tomorrow with their disgusting asses, which created those fuckers you call sirens that somehow manage to have mates who don't mind their disgusting living habitat. Don't ask how I know this because I won't explain, but let's say that a drunk grandfather is not the best person to tell you things.

I walked over to the cauldron and looked to ensure it was clean before dumping the soup in there. I used my magic to make a fire so I could heat my food. I went to Nyra, and I'd secret cabinet filled with booze that we kept from Salem because she loved to get drunk when she was feeling bored, which was all the time. I saw that there was a note that said,

For Amora ;)

I chuckled softly, took the bottle down, and raised it high as if to thank Nyra before opening it and taking a sip. Once my food finished heating, I put it into a bowl and set it on the table, and I placed the bottle in front while I grabbed a spoon.

"Thank you, Nyra," I murmured before digging in. After dinner, I washed the cauldron and the dishes I used before taking the booze that Nyra had given me along with another to my room. I set the other bottle on my nightstand and held the other close as I sipped it. Usually, when I was alone, I'd drink until I finished the bottle and fall asleep. I did this back at the Black Fang pack house, and I would drink an entire bottle of booze and then sleep. Jayden hated it, but I loved it because it was a great way to drift off.

Chapter Seventeen

It was finally the day that the Fae King and his son would come and get what they needed. I reminded myself from when I ate to when I got dressed to not fall for their charms and to remember that even if their words held promises, they would fuck me and leave me with a child. It helped me prepare for the worst because I didn't want to fall for their charms, even if the prince was a good-looking hunk. As for the marks on my body I received from Jayden, I healed them myself because I didn't want to look bad in front of them.

A knock sounded on the door as I got a drink of water. I took out the water and headed to the door. I opened it, and sure enough, there was a gorgeous man with long white hair, pointed ears, high cheekbones, medium heart-shaped lip, blue eyes that were so light that they were transparent, a lean build, and deep dimples. This other one was the same height as the first with the same features. It was hard to tell them apart when they looked like spitting images of each other.

"Hello, dear," The Fae King greeted. His voice was deep yet soft when he spoke to me, shocking because I've been around a bunch of deep, rough-voiced men all my life. It was refreshing to hear it, making me wonder why I didn't have a Fae as a mate.

"Hello, your highnesses," I greeted.

"I'm sure Nyra has told you why we dropped by to visit?" He asked.

"Yes, she has," I responded as I let them in. The prince watched me as I walked further into the kitchen, and I grabbed the bottle from the shelf and gave it to the King.

"Thank you so much, my dear," He smiled at me.

"You're welcome, sire," I smiled back.

"No need to be so formal, my dear," He laughed, "It makes me feel old in a way, especially when a beautiful young woman is speaking to me." See what I mean? They're charming, but they're the fuck boys/fuck girls of the supernatural community, but a compliment is a compliment. Besides, Jayden doesn't say shit to me. He didn't even say shit to me when he was pretty much beating my walls black and blue.

"Thank you," I smiled.

"Father, please stop flirting with her. You're far too old for her," The Prince spoke up. His voice was a little deeper than his father's, but it was still soft and gentle like his.

"I'm never too old to flirt with such a beautiful woman," He winked at me. I giggled softly.

"But it's a shame that you have a mate," The Prince said, "If you hadn't found one, then maybe we could've been together."

"Thorne, you and I both know that you'd court me without a care about my mate," I smirked.

"Well, can you blame a man for doing that? You are a very radiant and powerful woman who speaks her mind and doesn't let any man run over you. You are the very definition of beauty," Thorne, The Prince, smiled.

"Thank you, Thorne," I smiled back, "But flattery will get you nowhere until I see some action." He laughed.

"Of course, Amora," He said. The door to my house opened, and one of their guards was holding a bouquet of stargazer lilies, and he handed them to me.

"Thank you. These are very beautiful," I beamed.

"These flowers pale in comparison to your beauty," He responded. The same guard walked over to the King who had been watching us and whispered something in his ear.

"Well, the beautiful daughter of Bronwyn, we must take our leave. Nyra should be expecting a thank you very soon," The King informed me.

"I will, sir," I nodded. The king kissed me on the hand and walked out of my home with a grace that most dancers would envy.

"I'm sad to leave such a beautiful creature such as yourself," He put a finger under my chin. I smiled softly. He kissed the corner of my lips, and my cheeks lit up.

"However, I will invite you to join me in my kingdom," He said.

"And what will we do in this kingdom of yours?" I asked.

"It is a surprise," He replied.

"I look forward to it," I chimed. He chuckled and smiled at me.

"I bid you farewell, Amora," he murmured.

"Farewell." With that, he left my home. I walked to the door and watched as they went in their carriage with beautiful white horses that took a running start before disappearing with a bit of gold dust behind them. I guess I didn't heed Nyra's warning and allowed them to slip honey into my ear.

"So the Prince of the Fae has his sights set on you." I almost jumped out of my skin at my dad's voice. I saw him sitting at the table with a glass of scotch in his hands. There was an upside-down bottle on the table with a glass identical to his sitting next.

"Can you warn me when you visit?" I asked.

"What's the point in doing that when scaring you brings me so much joy?" He chuckled.

"You're terrible," I shook my head.

"And don't you forget it," He winked. I rolled my eyes as I put the lilies in a vase.

"What are you doing here?" I asked.

"Your Mother is away in Europe for three months for some type of council meeting, and Alan is off causing chaos in another dimension with your chaos, so I got bored and decided to come here," He answered.

"Thanks, Dad. I feel so much better learning that you only came here to visit because you were bored," I muttered.

"You know I didn't mean it like that, Amora," He said.

"I know, Dad. I'm just messing with you," I giggled.

"How is your mate bastard doing since he kicked you out?" He asked. A deep frown formed on my face.

"I don't know and don't care," I spat venomously.

"What did he do now?" He asked as I set the lilies on the counter.

"Nothing, except piss me off as usual," I mumbled.

"Why don't you just kill the bastard already?" He asked.

"Dad, no. That'll cause a war," I replied.

"Who cares? You'll have an army of demons behind you to help fight it," He said.

"You're making it sound like I'm going to do it now," I told him.

"Now would be a perfect time," He remarked.

"No, Dad. I'm not killing Jayden to appease your hunger for chaos and destruction," I said.

"A man has to eat sometime," He added.

"Well, go eat somewhere else," I said.

"Fine. I'll stop trying to encourage you to start a war, even though I hate that damn dog," He sighed.

"Thanks, Dad," I smiled.

"You're welcome," He grumbled.

"So, where's abuelita?" I asked.

"At home gossiping with her friends," He informed me.

"So that whole grandfather and Alan aren't home thing was an excuse for her kicking you out?" I smirked.

"Oh no. That wasn't an excuse. They're not home right now," he answered.

"Ahh. So she did kick you out," I chuckled.

"Yes," He muttered under his breath, "I don't see why when it's my castle."

"Technically, it's a family castle, but go off," I said.

"It became mine once I was crowned," He replied.

"Dad, it's still a family castle," I told him.

"Oh, hush and just feel bad for your father," He snapped.

"Alright. No need to get snippy with me, sonny," I said.

"Sorry, my little terror," He stood up and kissed my forehead. He sat back down and poured himself some scotch, and he turned over the other glass and ran some for me too.

"Ah, man. You guys broke out the scotch?" Eve complained as she walked into the house with a grocery bag. I used my magic to duplicate a glass-like ours. My dad poured some for her as she placed the grocery bag on the counter. She took a seat at the table.

"How have you been, Eve?" My dad asked.

"I'm doing alright. A little bummed I haven't found my mate yet," She sighed.

"Don't be so down about it, my dear. You'll find them someday," He assured her.

"I hope it's soon," She mumbled as she took the scotch to the head. She let out an 'ahh' and placed the glass on the table. My dad smiled and filled it again.

"I still can't believe you two have grown into such beautiful young ladies. Just yesterday, I was saving you, girls, from getting killed by some psychotic Fae on a killing spree," My Dad reminisced.

"That was one of those memories I didn't need to be brought up," Eve muttered.

"Well, you two shouldn't have been looking for trouble in the first place," He said.

"Don't include me in that. It was all her idea," Eve jabbed a thumb in my direction.

"The lies you tell," I mumbled under my breath.

"Oh, so it was your idea to look for him?" My Dad asked.

"Thanks a lot, snitch," I glared at Eve.

"Please explain why a nine-year-old had the bright idea of looking for a serial killer?" He raised an eyebrow at me.

"I wanted to see if I could kill him myself. Was that so wrong?" I responded.

"Yes, It is, considering how he almost killed the both of you," He told me.

"Well, you saved us, didn't you?" I said.

"I did, but had I not gotten there in time, you both would've been dead," He replied.

"Well, we're not so, thanks," I smiled. He sighed and rolled his eyes.

"You're the worst," Eve spoke up.

"I learned from the best," I gestured to my dad.

"I've never done something that could've gotten us potentially killed," he said.

"Las mentiras que dices," I muttered under my breath.

"Whatever. You're just making up stories," He rolled his eyes.

"¿De verdad estás tratando de hacerme ser un mentiroso ahora?" I inquired.

"It seems like he is," Eve chimed in.

"Oh, please. I have never done anything that has almost gotten us killed," he said.

"Sí tienes. Remember that time you took me to visit the vampires with you? Remember how you ended up pissing them off, which caused them to get mad and try to kill us?" I inquired.

"First of all, they were being assholes, and second, you didn't almost get killed," He waved me off.

"¿¡Dios mío!?" I exclaimed, "They tried to suck me dry, Padre!"

"Ugh! Fine. I'll admit that wasn't my best moment, but that was a one-time thing," He finally admitted.

"Padre, that was more than a 'una cosa del tiempo'," I shot at him.

"Fine. You got me," He sighed loudly, "Maybe I wasn't the best parent in those moments, but at least you vivió para contar la historia."

"Apenas," I muttered under my breath.

"Why did you come by with groceries?" My dad changed the subject.

"Hm? Oh, I wanted to come by and visit Amora. I was planning on staying over for the night since I know she'll probably get lonely," Eve explained.

"You're such a dulce girl," My dad smiled.

"Thank you, sir," She smiled back.

"Hey. por qué no puedes be more like her?" My dad turned to me.

"¿Qué? I am sweet, old man," I replied.

"Que seguro como el infierno wasn't you being sweet," he said.

"Oh, lo que sea, papá. Puedo ser sweet," I rolled my eyes.

"Mmm....not really," Eve said.

"¿Qué te know?" I asked.

"I know enough that you're not sweet," She shot at me.

"¿No necesitas lick your culo or something?" I countered.

"Oh, that's rich coming from you, the girl who couldn't even figure out how a phone worked for two years," She rolled her eyes.

"It's not my fault that my familia kept me fuera del bucle because we no tenía necesidad for them," I snapped.

"As entertainingly stupid as this conversation is between you two, I must take my leave," My dad spoke up.

"Why?" I asked.

"The vampires wanted to discuss something with me about our kingdoms," He informed me.

"Ohh," I nodded.

"Bye, Mr. V," Eve smiled.

"Goodbye," He kissed both of us on our foreheads before bursting into flames before our very eyes. A burn mark was left on the floor where he once stood, and I used my magic to get it out.

"Your family sure does love flashy entrances and exits," Eve commented.

"They all have a flare for dramatics," I said. She chuckled.

"So, what has your idiot cousin been up to since he kicked me out?" I asked.

"He's been working a lot, as usual, he's much crabbier too, and he's talking to this girl named Amber, who's from another pack. They've been getting close," She answered.

"How long have they been talking?" I asked

"They start two days after you left," she answered.

"He moves on quick," I muttered under my breath.

"Yeah, he does, but he's an idiot for not realizing how great you are, even though you have tried to kill him and members of our pack more than once," She said.

"Thanks, E," I smiled.

"You're welcome," She nodded.

Chapter Eighteen

It was supposed to be the day of my date with Thorne, but he had canceled because of important matters that he needed to attend to. He had told me this in person and apologized profusely, but I assured him that I understood that he had duties to his kingdom before he was crowned king. To make it up to me, he promised that we go on our date tomorrow around the same time, and he gave me a bouquet of lavender lilies. It was a sweet gesture, and I appreciated it so much. Unlike some people, he didn't get on my nerves or make me want to kill him every second, so there's a plus.

Speaking of important matters, my mother had messaged me an hour after he left to head over to the coven due to an urgent issue between two witches. The two were ready to kill each other over something one did. The entire argument ended up leaving two other witches injured and three others, including a young child, with minor bruises and scrapes. She asked me to handle this because she was away on business and felt that I was capable enough to deal with it on my own. She even told me that she would have one of the elders monitor me and ensure I didn't kill anyone out of frustration. I could see why she did that because I can get pissed off pretty easily, and there's no telling what I'll do.

"So, your mother is entrusting you to give your judgment over two witches who almost had a full-blown battle?" Eve asked as she lay on my bed.

"Ummm...yeah. She trusts me," I responded in a 'duh tone.

"I'm just asking because it seems a little worrisome to have you do that," Eve said.

"Whatever. I give fair and just judgment," I rolled my eyes.

"Amora, you almost killed some vampire like a month ago for not saying excuse me," She remarked.

"That was a one-time thing, Eve," I replied.

"A month before that, you almost killed one of the teenage members of my pack for getting smart with you, even though I've been wanting to do it for a long time," Eve added.

"So, you admit that she was a pain in the ass? Hm?" I smirked.

"Maybe that doesn't count, but the time you almost killed my cousin for even saying good morning to you does," She answered.

"First of all, he had pissed me off enough that morning, and second, he was skating sheet-thin ice," I responded.

"So, I guess the siren who looked at you funny was the same way?" She cocked an eyebrow.

"Don't even mention those disgusting singing bastards," I growled. Eve laughed while I scowled at her through the mirror.

"I don't see how your mom trusts you and your judgment when you can't even stay calm with others for a second," She chuckled.

"Oh, shut up," I hissed, "It's different when it's people who have known and loved you like your own family. You have patience for them and don't lose your temper, unlike with your pack, which I resent to this day and wouldn't mind seeing them burn."

"Understandable," She nodded, "The people there are shitty, especially my aunt and uncle."

"Does it ever feel weird just to insult them?" I inquired.

"No," She shook her head, "My pack was pretty terrible when I was a child, especially towards my parents because my dad isn't as strong as my uncle. They've mistreated my parents for as long as I can remember. My dad says it's because he was weak when he was a child, and everyone didn't like that, including my bastard grandfather. The treatment worsened after my uncle became alpha and even worse once everyone discovered that my dad was mated to my mom, an unwanted omega."

"Is that why you always hung out with me when you could?" I asked. It was surprising to hear this because Eve had never told me about this. It had always made me curious about why she would trash her pack in front of me, and I figured she would say it to me in her own time, and now she has.

"Yeah. My parents encouraged it because they didn't want me to suffer the treatment of our pack. They appreciated that you and your parents treated me nicely," She responded.

"Do they still treat you terribly?" I inquired.

"No. Not anymore after that day. You told Jayden to stop them," She answered, "There are still some rude remarks and other things being done, but it's not as bad as before."

"Did my parents ever know?" I questioned.

"They did," She chuckled, "Your dad almost decapitated my uncle in front of me until your mom stopped him. Now what she did was probably worse than what your dad did."

I wouldn't put it past my parents to be protective of Eve as much as they were with me, especially my mom. Her type of protection bordered between completely and utterly sadistic and murder.

"All she told me was that she showed him images so horrific and terrible in his mind that he would have nightmares for centuries to come. She didn't tell me what she showed him, but let's say my uncle wakes up screaming in his sleep," She replied. Depending on what my mom showed him, he will probably have nightmares until the day he dies. Anything worse than that probably would've made him kill himself. It's horrible, I know, but my parents are very protective of me.

"Hm. No wonder I would hear him scream in the dead of night," I said.

"Yeah. Everyone is pretty much used to it, so we all sleep through it," She shrugged, "He'll cry afterward, and my aunt will comfort him, but it's no use if it's an all-night thing."

"How long does it usually last?" I inquired.

"For like an hour or two, he's back to sleep. Nights, when it gets too unbearable for him, are long, and he ends up staying away till the next day," She responded.

"That's what he gets," I smirked. She chuckled.

"Mhm," She nodded.

"I'm surprised my mom didn't do anything to your aunt," I said.

"Oh, she did. While my uncle was screaming his head off from what she showed him, she chained my aunt down in Nazareth and forced her to look at people getting tortured horribly for a month our time," She replied.

"Oh wow. That's terrible," I chuckled.

"It was. My aunt had a mental breakdown afterward," She informed me.

"That's what happens when you make them angry," I smirked.

"It does. My aunt and uncle know not to anger your parents, and that's why they didn't do anything when your dad almost killed Jayden," she said. I snickered.

"Seriously?" I asked.

"Yeah. They were scared," She giggled.

"And you parents?" I questioned.

"Thoroughly entertained," She responded. We both laughed together.

"I guess you guys are used to our antics by now," I said.

"We are. Nothing you guys do surprises us for real, to be honest, and if it does, then we get over it and get used to it," She smiled.

"I'm glad. I don't think I can have a best friend who is always surprised and horrified by what I do," I murmured.

"I don't think you'd have friends at all if that were the case, especially after the shit you put me through," She replied.

"Oh, shut up!" I hissed. She laughed.

"Anyways, you ready?" I asked as I put on my black leather jacket. Eve was going to tag along with me while I went to handle my business. Other than the witch who would monitor me, Eve would be there to do the same. She was going to say some calming words to me so that I didn't lose it.

"Uh-duh. I've always been ready," She responded as she hopped off my bed. Eve had on all black like me since it was a traditional color for the coven wear worldwide. We wore other colors, but black was mainly what we wore around each other.

"Keep it up, smart ass, or else that tongue of yours will be no more," I said.

"Hush," She waved me off. We both walked out of my room and into the kitchen.

"So, how are we doing this?" She asked.

"Fire," I answered, "I want to make an entrance."

She let out a chuckle with a smile.

"Alright," She nodded. A candle in the kitchen had been lit, and I pointed my finger at the flame until it left the wick. I took my finger and raised it above my head, then waved it around like a lasso. Eve stood next to me and watched in amazement as my finger lowered, and so did the flame. The flame circled us in a spiral, and then we were engulfed in warm flames that didn't burn us.

When we arrived, the flames burst from the ground and disappeared into my skin like water.

"That never ceases to amaze me," Eve said.

"I bet," I smiled.

"Amora!" Eve and I looked to see a woman who seemed middle-aged coming towards us. The witch, Iracebeth, was supposed to watch me the entire time. The woman had an air of grace and regality around her that was expected of the elderly witches in our society. Most of them are former royals whose kingdoms have been long forgotten, but they still hold some weight within the community regarding our laws and other things that keep this coven together.

"Good afternoon, Iracebeth," I curtsied along with Eve. It was customary to bow or curtsy to the elders because it showed respect. Younger children didn't have to do it at all, but the older ones, like pre-teens and teenagers, had to.

"Rise, young one," She chuckled. She pulled Eve and me into a hug, and we hugged her back before pulling.

"So nice to see the both of you and how you've grown," She smiled.

"It's nice to see you again," Eve smiled back.

"My friend is right, Iracebeth. I've missed seeing your face," I said.

"You could see it more often if you'd just visit more often," She replied.

"That's true," I agreed, "I'll make sure to do it more often."

"That's my girl," She beamed, and her expression turned serious, "Now come. We must attend to the incident from earlier."

My expression became serious as well, and we followed her.

"Give me a rundown on what happened, Iracebeth," I said. She nodded.

"The incident from earlier was a terrible and ignorant one. I swear that these young ones get increasingly ridiculous every day as the centuries go by," She shook her head.

"What do you mean by that?" Eve inquired. Iracebeth looked at her with a deep frown.

"I mean that the young ones, around your age and younger, are becoming increasingly belligerent," she responded. "It's quite disappointing because back in my day, young ladies conducted themselves in a Lady-like fashion and weren't as vulgar as they are now."

"Oh," Eve nodded.

"But I understand that times have changed since I was a child, and women aren't as dependent on men as they were before," She responded.

"That is true," Eve agreed.

"What about the incident?" I inquired. If I let her keep ranting about young people, we'd be here forever, and I wouldn't be able to get things done, and that would be a pain in my ass, to be honest.

"Ah, Yes. The incident," She rolled her eyes.

"How bad was it other than the injuries the bystanders suffered?" I questioned.

"Other than the injuries, a few homes and buildings were destroyed. The ground is sunken from a spell one of them cast, and your mother doesn't know about this. Someone was killed in the crossfire," she explained.

"What?!" I looked at her. Eve looked at me worriedly. It was considered taboo to kill another one of your sisters, and it was rarely done without a reason. So to hear that one of our own was killed in the crossfire of some idiot's mistake pisses me off.

"The body is almost unrecognizable," She told me grimly, "It was quite horrible to witness, especially for the mother of the girl."

"Did you restrain them?" I asked. It was hard to contain the anger I felt right now.

"It took us a long time to do it because they were ready to kill each other. You know how hard it is for us to do that," She answered. A witch ready to kill was a hard one to restrain. I've witnessed that one too many times with my mother and Nyra, who is usually calm.

"I hope you used mountain ash," I growled.

"We did. We used it to restrain those two against the wooden stake," She murmured.

"Good because by the time I'm done with those two, they'll wish they were born," I snarled.

"Amora, calm down," Eve softly said. Silently, I nodded and let out a loud huff with a little bit of fire. We arrived at the middle of the town square, where two witches were chained to the stake with scratches and bruises on their faces. Many witches stood around and looked at them. When they noticed me standing there, they parted like the Red Sea and allowed me to walk through with Iracebeth and Eve flanking me.

A look of fear formed on their faces when they got a look at me, and it was satisfying to see. They better fear me now than ever before. Even though I didn't hear the full story, the thought of someone innocent being caught in the crossfire of their stupidity pissed me off.

I finally stopped before them, and they both looked at me with shame and fear. The expression I wore told them that I wasn't one to mess with, nor was I one to let them off easy. A grim and uncomfortable silence filled the air causing people to fidget.

Suddenly, they both burst into tears, causing me to stare at them harsher than before. It was no use in them crying because they knew what they had done was wrong and the possible consequences of their fighting. I moved an inch closer to them, and they began to shake as they cried harder than before.

"Irresponsible," I stated, "That's what you two are. Irresponsible."

"P-Pl-" I held up my hand to cut them off, and she did.

"Your excuses mean nothing. They mean nothing to those injured in the crossfire, nor do they mean nothing to the mother of the young girl killed here today," I snapped. Their crying was starting to annoy the shit out of me.

"What pisses me about this situation is that our fellow sisters had to suffer because of your transgressions. It pisses me off that you two didn't even think about the others around you who would suffer because of you. It pisses me off that one of our sisters is mourning the loss of her daughter. It pisses me off that you two are sitting here and crying your fucking eyes out while others are injured!" I spat venomously. They both flinched.

"Do you two realize the severity of your actions and what you have done? Do you realize how much pain and suffering you've caused our sisters within this fucking society? Do you realize how much destruction you've caused? Huh? Do you?" I bellowed. The ground around us began to shake, and many others began to cower in fear.

"You two have committed a horrible act against your sisters and your community. Since you two feel the need to fight over a man who will never really desire the both of you, you can live the rest of yours as undesirable, banished witches," I hissed.

"No! Please!" they both yelled out.

"Eve, you might want to close your eyes," I warned.

"I'm good," she responded. I reached into the middle of their chests, and they both screeched in pain. The sound was so loud that it would've damaged the eardrums of a human. Slowly, I pulled out two orbs, one was blue, and the other was yellow. This symbolizes the magic they had within their bodies, and now this magic was going to be stripped away by me, which means that I would take their powers into me. They ended up passing out from how intense the pain was. When it was over, I placed the balls of magic into my mouth and swallowed them.

Their magic coursing through my body felt like I was in a vibrating massage chair. The two girls unconscious bodies hung limply on the stake.

"Banish them to two separate deserted islands where no one can find them and where they have plenty of food and water. Make sure their memories are wiped of this community and replace them with false ones," I instructed Iracebeth.

"Yes, ma'am," She responded.

"Have someone else help you," I added. Iracebeth nodded and walked away.

"You are such a badass," Eve chuckled.

"Thanks," I smiled.

Chapter Nineteen

I was regarded by my mother. "What was your judgment on the entire situation?" My Mom asked. We were currently talking to each other through this vast, grand golden mirror within her house. It was the day after that incident since I made my final judgments on those two girls that had practically battled it out and eight hours since the repairs on the town had begun. A ceremony had been held for the girl who had died. Her body was laid on a wooden boat with a beautiful, vibrant flower bed to cushion her. Her body was adorned in a beautiful white lace gown, her head had a crown made of flowers on top, and a long white, sheer veil was placed over her entire body as it drifted down the river to a veil where all of the bodies of the dead must go. On the other side was a beautiful and pure place filled with many wonders. The spirits of those long gone walked around peacefully together. No living being could go there, and if they did, they wouldn't be able to return.

"Given the severity of their actions, I stripped them of their powers, had their memories replaced with false ones, and banished them to secluded islands that no one will ever find them on," I explained.

"How bad was the fight?" She asked.

"Very bad," I sighed, "There were some major and minor injuries on innocent bystanders, one person was killed, and the twin square was practically destroyed. It was a horrible sight to see."

"I bet. I don't see why these young girls don't just talk out their problems instead of being so quick to fight about them. Not every argument you get into is worth throwing your fists or using your magic," She ranted.

"It isn't, even though I can't talk since I am my father's daughter," I agreed.

"Yes, you are," She chuckled, "As for the one person who died, where are they buried today?"

"Yes, they were. They were buried earlier this morning at dawn, and it was a beautiful ceremony," I informed her.

"I wish I could've been there. Poor girl," She mumbled.

"The mother understands that you have duties overseas," I assured her, "You are the supreme, after all."

"My duties come after my people, even if it takes all my time and brain power," She sighed.

"I'm sure you'll drop by and comfort the mother," I murmured.

"You read my mind," She smiled. A calm voice murmured something to my mother, whose facial expression turned grim. My mother looked over at me.

"I must go. It seems as if a group of your father's subjects is attacking witches, vampires, Fae, wolves, and other creatures here in this country," She huffed.

"Oh no. Please don't blame him," I pleaded.

"You think less of me, Amora. I would never blame your father for the misdeeds of his people," She responded.

"There was that one time," I mumbled.

"I was justified that time," She told me.

"Whatever you say, mother," I giggled.

"Let me go before I end up choking you through this mirror," She smiled, shaking her head.

"Love you, Mom," I grinned.

"I love you too, my little terror," She responded. We both said goodbye, and the mirror returned to normal.

"How does this look?" I asked Eve. She was lying on my bed in a pair of Mom jeans, a tee that was tucked in, and a couple of mismatched socks. She looked up from the vintage playboy she was reading to look at me. I don't know why she looked at the printed smut when I was here.

"Are you sure you're not going to fuck this guy? If you are, then I'm not judging," Eve replied.

"I just might. If your cousin can have fun with his new girl, then why can't I?" I smirked.

"You're right," She smirked, "Have fun and make sure you use protection."

"And if I don't?" I gave her a mischievous smile.

"Oh, so you must want a half-demon, half-Fae baby?" She asked.

"I do," I giggled.

"It's quite odd to me how Fae can have children with anyone besides their mate," Eve remarked. Fae can indeed do that, so it's not uncommon to see them with creatures, not their species.

"Well, Fae, given that they fuck like rabbits, I'd say that it would make sense for them to reproduce because at least half of them will at least think before they fuck without a condom," I murmured. Eve laughed.

"I guess the pull-out game is weak," She joked.

"Shut up," I laughed. She joined in on the laughter as well.

"Since you said they fuck like rabbits, then I guess they reproduce like rabbits, too," She added.

"Oh gosh. That's so true that it's funny," I chuckled.

"Oh my gosh. Really?" Eve cracked up.

"Yes," I giggled, "You'll see a normal Fae couple with at least ten to twelve children in one household and maybe one more on the way."

"Oh gosh. They're worse than wolves, and we pop them out like crazy. That's why our packs have so many members around the same age," she sneered.

"Your Mom told me that the first week I stayed there. She said it was normal if I had at least ten of them," I murmured.

"Ten? Ten is for beginners in my species," She snorted, "Sixteen is for real wolves."

"So, I'm going to reject your cousin," I mumbled. Eve laughed.

"I wouldn't blame you, but from what I've witnessed with your parents, you're not too far behind in that department," she told me.

"Ew! Shut up!" I exclaimed. She began cracking up.

"If It were possible, I'm sure you would have siblings by now," She added with a smirk.

"Well, my mom is working on it," I mumbled, "As gross as it may sound, she's trying to figure out a way in which she and my dad can have another demon child."

"Isn't there a curse placed upon demons when mating with witches?" She asked.

"There is, but my mom has been trying to break it for years with Nyra. It's kind of a hard code to crack, but I'm sure in due time, there will be another child like me running around for the next few centuries," I explained.

"Aww. I wish I had siblings too, but my parents can't anymore since my mom had her tubes tied," Eve scowled at the wall.

"I forgot about that," I replied.

"They did it to be cruel, and I hate it. I still don't understand why my parents won't leave the pack," She shook her head.

"Can't you be banned from ever going to another?" I asked.

"Yes," She nodded, "But I don't mind anyway. I never wanted to be part of any of those packs."

"That's understandable. If your parents ever decide to leave the pack, you always have a home with my parents and me no matter what," I smiled, "Although I don't think you want to live with my dad."

"Oh, Gosh! Please don't suggest I live with your dad. I don't think I could keep my sanity there," She groaned.

"That's why I visit once a month our time," I chuckled.

"That's true," She nodded. My eyes traveled to the clock on the wall, and I gasped loudly.

"I'm late! I'm late! I'm late; I'm late, I'm late!" I exclaimed. Quickly, I slipped on the pointed-toe black heels and grabbed my purse. Eve laughed as I ran around like a chicken with its leg cut off. This shit isn't funny.

"I got to go!" I spoke.

"Are you wearing underwear?!" Eve called after me.

"Hell no!" I yelled back. She laughed loudly like a hyena. I walked through the fireplace and was instantly transported outside the Fae castle, where Thorne stood with a smile.

"You're late, my sweet," he teased.

"I'm sorry, Thorne. I was talking to my mum," I apologized.

"That's understandable," he chuckled. He held his arm to me, and I wrapped mine around it with a smile. We both began walking towards the castle together in comfortable silence. I decided to take in the scenery around me, and I had to admit that it was beautiful and grand. It was opposite my father's castle, just a black gothic-looking building. This one had a beauty that gave you a sense of peace and serenity.

"Your home is stunning," I gasped.

"Thank you, Amora. Although, I am sure my home pales compared to your father's," He murmured.

"My father's home is beautiful, no doubt, but yours is just magnificent, and it seems like such a peaceful place," I replied. We both looked at each other.

"Yeah, right," We both laughed. As we walked through the beautiful castle, Thorne told me a few funny stories from his younger days and now. It was quite amusing to hear him talk about his very embarrassing moments, and relieved because I wasn't the only one that made some mistakes when going to meetings with their parents.

"There has been one question on my mind for quite some time now, Amora," Thorne informed me.

"Yes, Thorne?" I asked.

"Are you and your mate still estranged?" He inquired.

"Yes. He's completely forgotten about me," I answered.

"He's an idiot for doing so. You're a lovely woman, and I, for one, would never forget about a woman like yourself," he told me. A small giggle slipped from my lips.

"Like I said before, Thorne. Words mean nothing unless action follows," I smiled. His eyes raked over my body for a moment which had me wet like Niagara.

"I did have dinner planned for us today, but I guess we can skip it," he conceded.

"Skipping meals is a bad thing, Thorne. You must eat something," I cooed seductively. Without another word, he secretly slipped his fingers under my dress and caressed my pearl before removing them. He put them into his mouth and sucked the juices off them with a low moan that almost had me gushing. He picked me up bridal style and carried me down a long corridor.

Tonight was going to be such a fun night.

Chapter Twenty

It was the day after my date with Thorne, and I was getting home after having breakfast with him and a few rounds in the shower and his bed until he had to go to a meeting with his father. He promised to drop by when he could before I left, and it made me feel all giddy, like a kid in a candy store. This was the first time I had felt true bliss outside of being with my family or Eve, and I was elated. If everything with Thorne goes well, I will consider rejecting Jayden as my mate.

"Eve! I'm back, and I have some great news!" I announced happily as I slipped off my heels at the door. Even though I was happy inside, it showed so much on the outside. For instance, I was doing something I had never done before: humming. I was buzzing like Julie Andrews in The Sound of Music, except I sounded less like a woman who exuded grace and beauty and more like a dying whale. It didn't matter what I said when humming because I was happy; that is all that mattered.

Soon, Eve came rushing downstairs urgently. When I turned to look at her, I noticed that she had a deep frown on her face. My smile faltered at her upset expression.

"What happened, Eve?" I asked. She hesitated as she thought of what to say and how to word it correctly so she wouldn't upset me. I knew it had to be bad if she acted like this, but I didn't realize how bad it would be.

"I don't know how to tell you this, Lani," She mumbled.

"What? Did something happen? Was anyone giving you a hard time?" I asked. Although many women and men in the coven adored Eve, some still didn't like her or her kind due to bad experiences, stereotypes, and other negative things they had seen, heard or witnessed.

"No. No one gave me a hard time, Lani. It's just that my cousin is here," she responded.

"What?!" I exclaimed, and my anger began to rise at her mentioning him being here. The house started to shake a little, and Eve looked at me worriedly.

"Amora, I know you two aren't on the best of terms, but please don't let yourself get too upset," She replied.

"And why not?" I spat venomously. "He was an insufferable jackass who irritated my soul and me every single second of every single day. You expect me to stay calm when he decides just to come to visit me after making it very clear that he wanted nothing to do with me?!"

"Amora, I understand your anger, and you have every right to feel this way. Frankly, if I were you, I'd feel this way as well, but you need to calm down and not let it get the best of you, or else you will do something you will regret," Eve told me. My anger calmed down a bit, and the house stopped shaking. I used my magic to repair any damages I might've caused so my mother wouldn't complain when she returned.

"Fine," I scowled, "I'll calm down, but the second he pisses me off is the same second he will die by my hands."

"I won't hold you back," she agreed.

"Thank you, Eve," I replied.

"No problem," she added.

"Now, where is that insufferable ass?" I asked.

"He's in the living room, but there is something else that you need to know," She answered.

"What?" I looked at her.

"He brought the girl he has been seeing," She replied truthfully. The nerve of this asshole to do that.

"And why in the hell would he bring her here?" I snapped.

"I don't know. He just said that she had every right to be here," She replied.

"Hm. Since he feels that way, let me get changed from these clothes," I informed her. Eve took one look at my attire.

"You weren't wearing that dress yesterday," She remarked. A grin appeared on my face this time as soon as she said that.

"No, I was not," I beamed. As gentle and innocent as Fae night looks, they are complete and total beasts in bed. Thorne ripped my dress straight down the middle and promised to buy me another dress, just like it, in many different colors. I was too horny to even give a shit about the dress, but it was nice that he would even say that. The outfit I was wearing now was a beautiful long white silk dress with a split going up to my thigh.

"Wait. Tell me everything while you get changed," She replied excitedly.

"You know I'll tell you every single thing you need to know," I smirked. We headed upstairs together, talking excitedly with each other while not giving a shit about the company downstairs. Once in my old room, I shut the door, and Eve plopped onto my bed.

"Tell me everything, and don't leave nothing out," she begged.

"Well, he showed me around the castle for a bit, and we talked. He's such a funny guy and charming too," I smiled dreamily, "He did have dinner planned for us, but we ended up just skipping it altogether because I needed some dick and he needed some pussy, so it was a win-win situation."

Eve giggled softly.

"It's cute how you guys seem to have hit off considering how his father, at some point, did want you to marry him," she mused.

"To be honest, I was a little skeptical of his intentions when he visited me, but I just looked through his mind and his father's and saw that they didn't have any plans to try and get me to be with his son. I guess he gave up on the idea when news broke out that your cousin and I were mates," I replied, picking out an outfit to wear.

"Well, if things with Thorne go in the right direction, then I suspect that you two won't be mates for long," Eve remarked.

"No, we will not," I agreed. Finally, I decided on an oversized sweatshirt and ankle boots. I used my magic to correct my hair and just let it fall onto my shoulder in its naturally curly state.

"So, are you going to see him again?" Eve inquired.

"He's dropping by later after his meetings," I answered.

"Ooh! I can't wait to meet him," she enthused.

"I'm sure you'll like him. He's a nice guy," I smiled.

"I'll be the judge of that," She replied. After I finished getting ready, we both headed downstairs together. When we got there, Jayden was about to touch something precious and ancient to my family while his girlfriend sat on the couch.

"Don't touch that. It's ancient and valuable to my family," I ordered. He moved away from it quickly and looked over at me.

"You kept us waiting," he frowned. A look of disbelief at the bullshit he just spouted came over my face, and I looked at Eve, who just gave me that same look as well.

"I don't know who the hell you're talking to like, but it isn't me, sis," I shot him, "You came to my home uninvited and unannounced like you owned the place when you don't. So miss me with that bullshit."

Eve snickered lowly right beside me while Jayden glared at her.

"I'm sure your mother wouldn't like you speaking to your guests like that," His new girlfriend spoke up. My attention was now on her, and I could tell instantly that she was the type to want to try people.

"Bitch, don't you ever fix your lips to talk about what my mother likes or dislikes. You don't know her from a can of paint, so keep your mouth shut, baby," I snapped. She made a 'humph' sound.

"Jayden, I can see why you kicked her out. She is so difficult," She told him. I glared at her menacingly, and suddenly, she began to choke. She clawed at her throat and gasped for air as it became difficult for her to breathe. Jayden rushes to her side quickly, but I used my magic to send him flying into a chair and bound him to it. Calmly, I walked over to blonde as she struggled to breathe. Her face went from blue to purple as she lay on the ground.

"Amora! Let go of me!" He angrily boomed.

"Silence," I flicked my wrist, and he went mute. He became angrier and struggled in the chair, and my attention was now on his bitch who sat here and tried disrespecting me in MY home.

"Listen here, you filthy little bitch. I do not take too kindly to disrespect at all, so the next time you fix your lips, talk down on me as if you are not in my house and territory. I will take you to Nazareth, where I will chain you up in his dungeon and torture you until you are a pathetic, broken repair worm who will have nightmares of what I will do to you. Do you understand me?" I threatened lowly. She slowly nodded with tears in her bugged-out eyes before I finally stopped. She coughed and gasped for air like a fish violently. Jayden was released from the chair, and he rushed to her side once again.

Calmly, I sat down on the Love seat across from them and crossed one leg over the other while Eve stood behind me.

"Either tell me why the hell you're here or get out. I have things to do and people to see," I seethed. Jayden glared at me.

"Well? I don't have all day."

Once she was okay, he helped her onto the couch, and they sat down.

"Eve get her some water," Jayden ordered in his alpha tone. Eve glared at him and headed to the kitchen. She came back moments later with some water, and instead of giving it to him, she slammed it down onto the table, causing a little of it to spill on there.

"Hey! Don't slam shit on that table," I told her.

"I'm sorry, Amora. I'll clean up the mess," she replied.

"Thank you," I nodded. Our attention went back to Jayden, who ensured she drank all the water. Eve took the glass when it was empty.

"This is what you're having my cousin do? Be a maid for you?" He growled.

"Didn't you hear her, dumbass? She said that she would clean up the water. God. I swear some people have a brain but don't know how to use it," I snapped. He glared at me.

"You don't get to sit here and say some bullshit about me when you were the one who just ordered your cousin to get this bitch some water like she was a damn maid. Don't you ever project the shit you do onto me," I snarled. Why did I let this fool dominate me when he's dumb as rocks? Who in the universe thought it was such a good idea to have us be mates with each other? They must've been bored out of their ever-loving mind to do so bullshit like this.

"Now tell me what the fuck you came here for, or else get out!" I seethed. He huffed loudly and looked at me seriously.

"Fine. I want you to reject me," he revealed.

"Okay," I nodded. A confused look came over his face at how quickly I said that.

"What?" he asked in disbelief.

"I said, 'okay.' I'll reject you," I responded. He was shocked at how quickly I made my decision, but it's not like the thought hadn't crossed my mind.

"Why are you so quick to reject me?" he inquired. It seems as if he wasn't expecting me to be this way. Maybe he thought I would put up a fight or something about it, but there was a fat chance of ever happening.

"I dislike you. Yeah, there was a point in time when we were living together when I had once liked you and considered making it work. Still, after you started to get on my nerves and piss me off every single fucking day, I didn't give a fuck about you or that damn pack," I explained, "From day one, my only concerns were Eve and her parents, not yours or those bastards within the pack. Hell, if I were pushed to it, I probably would've slaughtered just about every single one of you with no mercy whatsoever and spared Eve and her parents. One day, I was close to it but decided against it."

"So you mean to tell me that you have thought about this for a while?" He growled.

"I don't see why you're getting upset with me. You didn't even like me either, and I could tell that there was some resentment forming towards me," I responded, "If you had been trying to make it work, then you would've made an effort as I did, but you didn't so here we are."

"I don't know why you're putting up a front," the bitch said, "We all know that you still miss him."

"I'm not gonna even choke you this time," I spat. I uncrossed my legs and leaned forward. My hand turned black, and my nails grew. Slowly and carefully, I drew a circle on the coffee table and chanted a summoning spell. Soon, a demon appeared and looked human, but we all knew it wasn't. Usually, the demons with horrible reputations took the forms of humans or other seemingly mundane creatures before showing others the real horror behind their disguises.

"Trata con ella," I mumbled.

"Sí, señora," It responded.

"Don't kill her just yet," I ordered. It nodded obediently.

"Ugh. I hate those demons," Eve complained. Jayden growled at the demon as it approached his bitch, but it paid him no mind and dragged her off. Jayden tried lunging for it, but all it took was a flick of my wrist, and he was thrown back into the seat. The bitch screamed and cried out in horror as she was dragged away from my home to somewhere secluded where she would be dealt with.

"They get the job done," I murmured.

"I guess," She sighed, hopping over the couch. She sat down beside me and faced her cousin.

"You traitor! I can't believe you're siding with her," Jayden spat.

"It's not exactly siding if I'm staying out of harm and not pissing off my best friend," Eve mumbled.

"That's kind of the definition of siding," I told her. She chuckled.

"Whoops," she shrugged. I let out a laugh and shook my head.

"You will be punished for your transgressions," he growled at her.

"Actually. I thought I wouldn't be punished because I'm leaving the pack," Eve responded. A shocked expression came over his face. I could tell he wasn't expecting that at all, but how long did he think he and his pack's mistreatment of Eve and her parents would go on? How long did they think they could continue belittling these people daily?

"What?! You can't do that! I won't allow you to," He hissed.

"You can talk about how you won't 'allow it or not, but this is my decision, and I'm sticking to it," Eve responded, "I am sick and tired of seeing my parents being mistreated because of things they could not control, especially my father. It gets on my fucking nerves to see you assholes do shit like this because, without my parents, this pack would fall apart at the seams."

Jayden listened silently and angrily as she spoke. I could feel his anger just radiating off him.

"Who do you think has been managing the finances when your dad was out spending money on frivolous shit? Who do you think was taking of the children who have grown into adults today? Who do you think was teaching half of the women in the house how to cook and clean properly?" Eve questioned, "Who do you think was running around helping in the infirmary when people were sick or injured? Who do you think was helping to train you and your fucking friends to fight? Who do you think was helping you all wipe your asses?"

It was about time that Eve finally got these things off her chest. It's been a long time coming for her to do so, and I'm happy that she is so she can leave that damn pack.

"MY PARENTS! My parents were the ones who did everything for this pack and still got treated like shit by the very same people they were helping!" She hissed, "It's time my parents and I leave this ungrateful pack for good and live as if we're not walking on eggshells."

"Even if you do leave, where are you going to live? You guys have no money or jobs, and you have nothing," Jayden smirked.

"That's where you're wrong. For a century, my dad has been the owner of a billion-dollar company that he's had since 1918, and he's been the sole, anonymous owner of it without your father, my uncle, knowing a damn thing about it. He's made so much money from it that he doesn't even need to work for the rest of his life," She explained, "In short, my parents and I can leave any time we want because we're going to be living the good life while you guys possibly spiral into the pits of debt and despair."

The room fell silent for a moment as Jayden soaked in the information.

"I guess that's all that needed to be said. Your cousin is leaving the pack along with your aunt and uncle," I murmured, "So let's get started."

With a snap of my fingers, the demon returned with the disrespectful runt he called a girlfriend, which was now a sobbing, broken mess. It threw her right at his feet, and

Jayden kneeled to comfort her. The demon took a knee right near me before vanishing.

"Jayden Black, I, Amora Gonzalez, hereby reject you as my mate," I firmly stated. The rejection of your mate wasn't painful at all, and it was more like a pinching feeling that didn't hurt.

"Amora Gonzalez, I, Jayden Black, hereby accept your rejection," He responded. I nodded.

"Good," I nodded. Eve stepped up to him.

"I, Eve Black, hereby officially resign from the Black Fang pack and declare myself a rogue," Eve stated.

"I, Jayden Black, accept your resignation," Jayden replied.

"Now that that's done," I began. "Get out. Take your little bitch too."

He glared at me and helped the girl up before leaving with her. Eve plopped onto my couch with me and let out a sigh of relief.

"So, do your parents know you're leaving?" I asked.

"Hm? Oh, they already resigned from the pack yesterday. They were waiting on me," she answered.

"You serious?" I inquired.

"Mhm," she smiled, nodding.

"Good for them. I guess you guys are going house hunting now?" I questioned.

"We already have a house," she responded.

"You do?" I looked at her in surprise.

"Uh-huh. My dad's had it for over a decade, and he's been waiting for the right time to live in it," She murmured.

"Wow. That's great," I smiled.

"I know, right," She chuckled, "Now all that is left to do is just take it easy."

"I heard that," I agreed. We both sighed contently as we sat back on the couch together.

Chapter Twenty-One

I sighed bitterly. "Why are there so many reports here?!" I exclaimed, "Esto es demasiado."

Iracebeth chuckled softly with a smile as she set yet another stack of reports onto the desk. I was practically dying of boredom. Looking over statements, managing finances, ruling with a sense of justice and kindness, and keeping our land well-maintained were very important to our coven because these things kept us from falling into the pits of debt and despair. It was the Supreme's job to do all this since she was the head of the coven, and it was her duty to ensure everything was in order. If the supreme didn't know how to do this, the coven fell apart entirely.

Did the supreme do this for all branches of the coven? Just for a few, and that was it. Other departments of the coven had trusted, reliable, and intelligent people who helped them manage their finances. Was it an easy job? No, but it paid off in the end when we could not spiral into debt and destruction. Without someone reliable to manage them, we were a mess, and we wouldn't have all the other ingredients we needed to make potions, cast certain spells, and perform certain rituals we couldn't find on our land.

Aside from managing finances for the coven, I also had to help my dad with problems with a group of demons causing trouble in the human territory. Those fuckers possess human bodies and cause all types of chaos. After getting a call from some hunters, my dad asked me to handle it since I handle the situation within the coven, so we'll. He also tested me on how well I could rule the demon world. I accepted the challenge, but I had to finish managing finances with the help of Iracebeth and Eve, who was very good at things like this too.

"We only have ten more things to look over," Eve murmured. A loud groan exited my mouth as I threw my head back.

"I need to get through this now so I can go deal with those fuckers," I snapped impatiently.

"You have a responsibility to this coven to review our financial reports for this week, and you can't just leave in the middle of them," Iracebeth responded, smiling. She had been smiling, laughing, and enjoying the boredom while also reminding me about my responsibilities towards this coven.

"Can we at least take an hour's rest so I can go deal with those guys? It's only a matter of time before they start causing even more shit," I yawned. "And you know how those damn hunters are when nothing is done."

The room fell silent as Iracebeth contemplated letting me go for at least an hour. Hopefully, she would let me go so I could leave and return as quickly as possible. If not, my dad will have to deal with it himself.

"It's fine, Iracebeth."

The familiar voice of my mother caused me to jump out of my seat practically. I wish she had not just done that because I almost had a heart attack, and supernatural creatures cannot have those as much as many would like to think.

"Alright, Amora. You have exactly one hour, and that's it. Come back as soon as possible," Iracebeth conceded.

"Yes, ma'am," I replied. I turned to my mother, whose image was floating in the air.

"Warn people next time when you do that. I almost had a heart attack," I scolded.

"Sorry, sweetie. I keep forgetting not to do that," She chuckled, "My mother always did tell me to warn people."

"It's good every once in a while to scare the piss out of your child," Iracebeth remarked. My mother laughed while I grumbled something incoherent under my breath.

"I'll get going now. I'll be back within an hour," I informed, reaching into my pocket. I pulled a small miniature broom between two fingers on each hand and stretched it out until it became a full-sized broom. My broom was always with me, although I never needed to use it. Today was an exception because I wanted to try out this speed rune my grandmother taught me a few days ago that makes you go into hyperspeed. The hyper-speed rune makes you feel like you've jumped from point A to point B within seconds.

"Be safe and make sure you don't cause any destruction. I don't want to hear that bastard's complaints," my mother warned. My mom and the new head of the Hunters organization aren't exactly on the best terms. Remember when I said that one of the kids in elementary school had bullied me? Well, the new head of the Hunters organization is his father. He hates my parents, especially my dad, after what they did to his shithead son. His son shouldn't have messed with fire because he did get burned.

"I promise not to cause any," I assured her.

"Good. Now be careful and good luck," my mom demanded.

"Thanks. I'll be back later," I mounted my broom. I grew out my nail, causing it to turn black, then cut myself hard enough to draw blood on my wrist. I scrawled the rune on my broomstick with my blood, and it flowed bright red and embedded itself in my broom. I waved goodbye before leaving.

Within seconds I was in Atlanta, Georgia, where the conflict was happening. This was where the headquarters for the Hunter organization was based. As soon as my foot planted onto the ground, hunters appeared all around me. They held their guns in their hands with special bullets that could take down all supernatural creatures and humans.

"State your name, your species, and your purpose for being on our land," One of the Hunters ordered. Silently, I shrunk my broom back to its original state before, then shoved it into my jacket pocket. The hunters waited for me to give them the information they needed, but I ignored them to brush off the tiny wood pieces stuck to the black midi dress I was wearing. I could tell they were getting impatient because one of them growled loudly.

Finally, I gave them the attention they desperately needed.

"My name is Amora Gonzalez, and I am here by the request of Gordon Archer, the head of the Hunters organization, as an official representative of Valrick Gonzalez, the king of Nazareth. Due to circumstances involving subjects of mine terrorizing your people," I informed with an air of authority in my voice. The sound of laughter caused me to look to my right, where a man with broad shoulders, a very muscular body, and black hair walked towards us. The group of hunters parted like the Red Sea to make way for him.

"Who would've thought that the demon girl who practically terrorized me when we were children would grow up to be like this."

I cocked an eyebrow at this strange man who talked like he knew me, but soon I chuckled at realizing who he was.

"Who would've thought that the sniveling, rude little bastard who dared to pick on an innocent little girl would become one of the most dangerous people in the world," I grinned devilishly. This was the head of the Hunters organization's son, Davy Matthews. He had become very handsome over the years, and he had his father to thank for that because his mother was two wine glasses and a pack of cigarettes away from looking like a total and complete hag.

"How long since we saw each other, Davy?" I smirked.

"About three years, but I guess three years is all it takes for you to forget a familiar face," He replied.

"Sorry, hon. I've been a little preoccupied with a few things," I smiled.

"Like what? Boning your mate, the alpha king?" He teased. I shook my head with a slight chuckle.

"I did bone the piece of shit, but I rejected him a few days ago," I murmured.

"Can't say I'm surprised. A bitchy little girl like you is going to grow old and miserable," He shot at me.

"Oh, what about you, Mr. Killer? How's that ex of yours?" I countered.

"You know what happened to Catherine, you piece of half-demon garbage. You were the one who ran her off," He responded. Another smirk appeared on my face at the mention of her name. Davy and I hadn't seen each other in three years since I tracked him down during college after some dastardly prank he pulled on me. I ended up seducing the bastard and his girlfriend at the time "accidentally" walked in on me riding his dick and moaning like a bitch.

The entire thing was hilarious because she stood there and watched as I fucked her man. I even winked at her ass which caused her to get angry and try to charge at me, but I ended up using my magic to blow her backward into a wall outside the room, then locked the door before continuing my little payback against Davy. After that, they broke up courtesy of me, and I gained a little fucked buddy before Davy broke it off to train with his father.

Was Davy mad about it? Not really, because he had been planning to break up with the girl, so I guess it was a win-win situation for us. However, whenever we saw each other, we constantly insulted each other like we're doing now. It was our weird little friendship, but it worked for us.

"Let's not get too comfortable reminiscing on your shitty deeds. Let's get down to business," Davy stated, becoming serious. I did the same and nodded.

"My father gave me the gist of the situation at hand, and I must say that I grasp the situation. I assure you that I won't cause any destruction to your territory and that I'll deal with these demons any way I see fit," I informed him. Davy nodded.

"Good. I'm glad I don't have to spend time briefing you on the details," He replied.

"As for your priests, how are they holding up?" I asked. Concerning demons, priests were the only ones who could expel them from human bodies, but they couldn't destroy them and could restrain them in specific containers.

"Two of them are unconscious with a few minor injuries, but nothing too serious," He replied.

"Any children involved?" I questioned.

"No. Just a young adult," He answered.

"What is their age?" I queried.

"Twenty-one," He replied, "Why do you have to know the age?"

"Because when it comes to demons, strength depends on age," I answered. This was a very true fact that I learned from Alan and my grandfather one time when my parents, Nyra, my abuela, and Salem were off on important missions. Demons who possessed humans put only one factor in mind: age, and the age of the human you controlled were also linked to your strength.

Teenagers and young adults were the main ones to be possessed because of their age, while adults in their mid-thirties to mid-fifties were in that area. Anyone after the early fifties was not common because they had a ten percent chance of surviving a possession. You'd be pretty stupid to possess an older man or woman. As for controlling infants and toddlers, you'd have to be a complete and total bastard for doing it because those are innocent children.

It was against Nazareth's laws to even do that in the first place, and my great-great-great-great grandfather made that law. After all, he sympathized with humans in that same aspect because he knew what it was like to lose a child over a horrible deed done by a demon.

"So the younger they are, the stronger they are?" Davy asked.

"Pre-teens, teenagers, and young adults are more likely to be possessed due to strength. As for children and the elderly are more susceptible to mental possession by demons," I explained.

"What is mental possession?" Davy questioned.

"It's where a demon will take a part of itself and turn it into something small like a fly that will go into your ear undetected and allow it to plant itself in your brain where it will have you do or say things that you wouldn't normally do," I answered. "Do you remember Gregory James from third grade?"

"How could I forget? He murdered his pregnant mother by stabbing her and pushing her down a flight of stairs in their basement," Davy spat.

"Gregory was possessed at the time," I replied.

"Really?" he asked in surprise.

"Yes. My grandfather and my mentor had to expel the demon from his mind. Oh yeah, and his mother and baby sister aren't dead," I murmured.

"What? But the coroner said-"

"My Mom had revived her and the baby in her belly that day. She created another body in place of his mother's and another in his. She even gave their entire family a new identity, which allowed them to assume a new identity in Greece, I think," I explained.

"Wow. Just when I thought your parents were terrible people," he remarked.

"Don't make me consume your soul," I warned him. He chuckled with a coy smile.

"I'd like to see you try," he challenged. A small smile formed on my features for a split second before my serious expression returned.

"Let's get back to the topic at hand," I murmured. He nodded with an expression that mimicked mine.

"Now tell me where the teenager is so I can get the demon out of them," I demanded.

"It's best if I lead you there," he responded. I nodded and followed him to where he was taking me. We had to go through so many security clearances to get to where we needed to that it wasn't funny. It was just plain irritating. You could tell that these people didn't play when it came to their own, and we didn't either. He finally led me to a metal door.

"May I?" I asked. He nodded and allowed me to use my magic to pass through the door. When I got inside, I saw a handsome hunk of a guy lying in the middle of the room, strapped to a hospital bed like a common animal. The man in question was pale with sunken eyes, dull chestnut brown hair that clung to his forehead, well-rounded lips that were a light pink, an aquiline nose, nice big hands, high cheekbones, thick eyebrows, nice sized ears, and muscular and toned body.

I walked towards the bed and ran my finger along the poor guy's leg. If I weren't with Thorne, I'd take him to hell and back in just one night. Who am I kidding? I could do it now since Thorne has concubines that he's had since he was two hundred years old. It wouldn't kill me to have one as well, and it's not like I'm going to even take this guy seriously in a romantic sense. My finger ripped up his leg towards the end of his hospital gown.

Without so much as any hesitation, I lifted the gown to see what he was working it. A gasp escaped my throat.

"I knew it," I hissed to myself triumphantly, "I knew his dick was big, and I just knew it."

It was just the right size. So thick and long that it looked like it could have a bitch walking zigzag for a month. This demon needed to be expelled now, for sure. My right hand began to transform into my black demonic form with red veins. I took my finger and cut my healed wrist once more. Blood began to drip, and I dipped my black nail into it. I turned to the man and drew an incantation on him that expelled the demon. He gasped loudly, and his body arched off the bed and against the restraints.

A black cloud began to deep out of his body and behind me. I used my magic to create a barrier around the entire facility that didn't allow the demon to escape. If they did try to, they would go directly to my father, who would deal with them for breaking one of our family's laws. The young guy's color returned, and he passed out for good on the bed.

"So you think you can-" The demon began to say until it saw me. A look of fear and shock came upon their features.

"I swear every single fucking time you bastards cause trouble, you never think of the consequences," I murmured, turning to look at it. I began to advance towards it, and it backed away in fear.

"You little assholes think that we won't find out that you're wreaking havoc for no reason and causing all this chaos without any orders whatsoever, but we do," I hissed. "We get pissed off every single time you fuckers show insubordination, especially my father."

As soon as I mentioned my dad, he began to cry like the little bitch he was. Understandably, he would feel this way because my dad was ruthless in punishing lawbreakers.

"Best believe that when I'm through with you, you'll be sent straight to him with your little friends," I maliciously grinned, "You'll all be wishing that I had dealt with you.

Chapter Twenty-Two

"Amora, I need to go over to the Black Fang pack for me," My Mom informed me from the mirror. It was another day without my mother, and I was still the substitute leader for the coven until she got back. It seemed she wouldn't be back any time since her trip had extended to another two weeks on top of the month that had been added.

It was a little tiring for me to do all this work she usually does, but I was pretty much used to it. Since I've been swamped, Thorne has been coming to me the entire time to spend some time with me and to give me a break so I would not crash. As for my concubine, he's also been a great stress reliever, so it's safe to say that I haven't completely lost my mind over the amount of work I have to do.

"Okay. What do you need me to do?" I inquired.

"Well, I need you to attend this meeting I was supposed to have with him today. It is a completely professional meeting involving our treaty with them, and it's us updating it," She informed me.

"Are we going to be the only ones there?" I asked.

"No. The other alphas of the branches of his pack around the world are going to be witnesses to it," She answered.

"Do I need protection?" I questioned as I pulled on a form-fitting strapless midi dress and slipped on a pair of high, thick-heeled sandals.

"No, you don't, but take Eve with you to calm you down. Getting angry in a room full of alphas isn't the smartest choice, especially when you are just one singular witch," She replied truthfully.

"If that's the case, why aren't any witches going with us?" I inquired.

"When we signed this damn thing during your great-great-great grandmother's time as ruler, they asked that we don't bring anyone unless it was a declaration of war. We agreed to these terms because we wanted peace as soon as possible," She explained, "It's stupid, I know, but this is the only way for us to keep the peace as we've done for centuries."

"Tradition is tradition," I mumbled as I threw on a black leather jacket. I took my hair down from the messy bun and let it flow down my soldiers, and my fingers ran through it to relieve some tension.

"There's a meeting I have to attend in a few minutes. Let me know how it goes today," She informed me.

"Okay, Mom," I responded.

"Thank you, sweetie. I love you," she cooed, blowing me kisses.

"Love you too, Mom," I smiled. The image disappeared, and my door opened to reveal Eve standing there.

"Eavesdropping?" I inquired with a chuckle. She giggled softly with a smile.

"It's not eavesdropping if you have ten times the sharing of a dog," She responded. We both began laughing at our small banter.

"Since we're going to be in a room full of bad-tempered men, I just need you to calm me down before I murder them all in cold blood," I instructed. She nodded as she became earnest.

"Do I have to hold back against you?" She asked.

"No. You're going to need to use all your strength," I responded, "Don't go easy on me just because we're friends."

She chuckled darkly with a smirk on her face.

"I never go wash on you," She remarked. A crooked grin appeared on my face at the sound of that.

"Good."

We arrived at a large clearing through the fireplace at exactly nine at night. The clearing was where we would meet with the many alphas from the different packs worldwide, plus the Alpha King.

"Any idea where the meeting is held?" I asked.

"My father told me that there is a stone well we have to go to that will open up once you have stuck your hand through the opening between the two stones on the bottom," She answered.

"And what else do I do?" I questioned.

"All he told me was that it was going to be painful," She replied.

"Well, that's not any help, but I'm grateful he told you these things," I mumbled.

"Me too. Kind of makes you wonder why he was not the alpha instead of my uncle, who really and truly didn't know shit," She agreed.

"I've always wondered that," I responded. She chuckled softly as we began walking through the clearing. The full moon shined down as we started our trek through the silent yet beautiful field. Fireflies danced around us as we walked, which was a delightful thing to witness. We finally reached the stone wall, and I walked over toward it. I crouched down and stuck my hand between the two rocks on the bottom. A sharp pain caused me to wince slightly as I pulled my hand out.

The stones began to shift entirely and split open down the middle. The ground shook a little causing nearby birds to fly away in fear. Stairs soon began to rise from the split, and the water inside the well started draining. It was a fantastic sight because I had never witnessed anything like it. You would think I wouldn't be impressed with the things I've noticed, but I am.

Once the stones finished shifting, Eve and I began descending those stairs. Lanterns along the walls lit up as we walked, and our steps echoed, alerting whoever was down there that we had arrived. When we made it to the last step, a handsome guy, who I could tell was a wolf, held his hand to me, and I took it with a small smile. He smiled back at me softly as he helped me to walk down steadily. He did the same for Eve as the gentleman he was.

"Who would have thought that one of you boys had the common decency to be a gentleman to little ole me," I smiled at him. He chuckled softly, giving me a dazzling smile.

"Despite our species' distrust of witches and hatred of witches, I still find the time to be a true gentleman to any beautiful woman I come across," He replied.

"You are so cute that I could just eat you up," I smirked. He laughed this time at my compliment.

"The only person who is going to be eating is me," He flirtatiously stated. My slut radar began to go off as I looked at him. My radar told me that sleeping with him would be the best thing to ever happen to me, and so did my digging into his mind.

"After this, you can-"

"Before you two get any more carried away, I must remind you both that there is a meeting we have to attend," Eve spoke up for the first time in a while. The guy and I gave Eve a " so " look before turning back. She rolled her eyes and grumbled something under her breath.

"-like I was saying, I can either come to where you are staying, or you can come to my place. The choice is yours," I told him.

"And if I declined your offer?" He asked. I cocked an eyebrow at his statement.

"Now, why would you go and do that?" I inquired. He laughed softly.

"I'm just trying not to get your hopes up," He replied.

"Declining my offer is the biggest mistake you could ever make in your life, especially for me, because I'll miss out on a chance to see your skills," I told him.

"I don't know how to feel about being used for that," He smiled.

"I'm only dishing out what you men give to us women daily," I responded, "Is that so wrong?"

"I have no objections to that," He nodded.

"I'll be waiting for your answer," I seductively cooed. He licked his lips and looked at me with a lustful look. I kissed his lips softly before walking away with Eve, who sighed right behind me as she followed.

"You never miss a chance to flirt with any good-looking guy you come across," She remarked.

"I can't help it. They're all just handsome that I want to devour them sexually," I told her.

"I'm going to need you to find some new words to describe what you want to do," She muttered.

"There is nothing wrong with my words," I rolled my eyes.

"There's a lot of things wrong with them, and what about Thorne? How does he feel about you doing what you usually do?" She asked.

"Thorne is fine with it as long as he's the one that I always come home to and vice versa," I replied, "You know how Fae get with their sex drive."

"You two are the definition of an open relationship," she snorted.

"Most supernatural relationships are like that," I told her, "My grandparents were like that at some point."

"And what happened to that?" Eve inquired.

"Hm? Oh, my grandfather got one of the women he slept with pregnant twins or something like that. My grandmother didn't want any more children running around, so she put an end to it," I explained, "My two uncles you met are those children."

"Ohh," Eve nodded. We continued walking until we came upon large metal doors. With a flick of my wrist, they opened slowly to reveal a group of prominent and muscular men chatting. A gasp was released from my throat at the faces of half of them, and they heard the noise and turned to face me—the half who I recognized all looked at me lustfully.

"Oh, bitch," Eve cursed from beside me. I knew that she knew that half of these guys starting at me were once people I either fucked, dated, dated, and fucked, or still fuck to this day. Just seeing all these guys in the same room felt awkward, but at the same time, it didn't because a few of them were good friends with me and had mates.

"Excuse me, gentlemen," Eve closed the doors quickly and turned to glare.

"Bitch, why is it that you end up fucking half the room every time we go somewhere?" Eve hissed at me, and all I could do was shrug while she made a feral growl of irritation.

"I have no problem with you getting fucked, but I have a problem with meeting them every single time at mandatory meetings and treaty signings," Eve snapped, "Either get it the fuck together, or else I'm going to fucking kill you! Stop fucking important leaders!"

My head was ashamed at her words as if I was a child getting scolded by her mother.

"I'm still fucking Thorne," I mumbled. She brought her hand down on my head hard.

"Except him, dumbass," She replied.

"Ow!" I yelped, "You didn't have to do that, you jackass!"

She kicked me hard in my backside with a glare, and I glared at her as I rubbed my ass. She opened the doors once more, with me still shooting daggers at her with my eyes. The men all turned to us again, and most of their faces held amusement.

"The fuck y'all looking at?" I snapped. A few of them chuckled while others growled at me out of anger, with their thoughts of fucking me into submission present in their minds.

"Quit being rude," Eve smacked me upside the head. As I looked away, a loud huff made its way out of my lips.

"Sorry," I mumbled.

"Louder," She ordered.

"I'm sorry for being rude. Please forgive me," I told them all loud and clear.

"Wow. Who knew that the little demon girl had some manners, eh?" A familiar voice said. I recognized the voice as Calvin, an arrogant alpha from Canada, remarked. A glare came upon my features at his statement. Calvin was a bastard who fucked me in the backseat of his car after I had disrespected him on his territory and made sure that I knew who I was talking to. I held my tongue each time I saw him because sex with him was like having sex with a literal demon. This is coming from a half-demon.

He was so demonic and sadistic that it was hard even to take control. Thinking about it tingled and irritated me simultaneously because he ensured I couldn't walk for two weeks. This isn't the worst thing he’s done to me, but that's another story.

"Hi, Calvin," I greeted. To be safe, I'm going to be nice to this fucker just so my legs can be secure. He smiled smugly at me, and I looked away so that my animosity for this asshole didn't show on my face. Most of the guys in here had looks of confusion on their faces for why I was being so nice to him and so submissive, but it was none of their damn business, to be quite honest.

"So, you finally arrived?" Jayden questionned from behind me. An expression of irritation formed on my face, and I turned to face the bastard who was the leader o the entire thing.

"Yes, I have. Problem with it?" I asked.

"Considering how you prioritized flirting with a lowly omega rather than coming here first, I'd say yes, I have a problem with that," He replied.

"Oh fuck off. Me flirting with the guy has nothing to do with this treaty signing, so get your fucking head out of your ass, and let's get this shit over with," I snapped, "Just being in the same room as you is enough to make me want to gouge my eyes out."

He narrowed his eyes at me and stepped closer to me. My eyes held his gaze as a way of saying that I won't back down, no matter how intimidating he made himself out to be.

"Need I remind you of the last time you had the misplaced courage to disrespect me?" he threatened in a low voice. "In front of all these men who are dying to get their hands on you?"

"I apologize for my behavior," I mumbled low enough for him and only him to hear.

"Good girl," he smirked at me, the bastard.

"Let's get this meeting started," Jayden announced. Eve walked over to me with a look of concern on her face.

"What the hell was that?" She hissed lowly. I shook my head at her to say that I did not want to talk about it.

The signing of the treaty was pretty much a breeze, with a few updated rules here and there, but nothing too serious. We signed it together, and soon the meeting was over, and I was so happy about that. After the signing, Jayden told most of the alphas in the room to head to his pack house so he could speak with me, and they all obeyed. I had Eve do the same because I also needed to talk to him. As for Calvin, that slippery snake, he slipped me his new number before leaving with everyone else.

Once those metal doors closed, silence filled the room.

"What did you want to talk to me about?" I asked. Jayden rolled up the treaty and placed it inside a long capsule. He set the pill down on the table and looked at me.

"I wanted to talk to you about my girlfriend, well, ex-girlfriend now," He responded.

"What about her?" I looked at him.

"You successfully ran her off after I visited your home, and she's scared out of her mind to even come to our territory. Her father, the former alpha of the Bastille pack, wants your head and will do anything to have it. He sent his twin sons, who are the alphas of the pack currently today, and they are awaiting their chance to take revenge," He explained. That statement made a malicious grin split my face and made it even more demonic than when I transformed. Jayden looked at me blankly, but I could tell he was worried about the outcome behind that.

Once you get me started, I'll never stop until I am satisfied, and he knows. After months of living with me, he knows how I get when it comes to fighting or torture. It makes the demonic blood running through my veins excited with the thought of causing the chaos and destruction I feed off.

"If they want to smoke with me, they can pull up and get it. Handling belligerent dogs is my specialty," I replied. Jayden stood from the table and walked over to where I leaned, and he moved in front of me and made a shield with his body.

"You haven't changed one bit," He remarked.

"Nor have you," I responded, "How is your whore of a mother? Still sucking off anything with a cock?"

He chuckled darkly for a moment as he looked at me with a smirk.

"And that is the exact comment that had you surrendering yourself to me," He ran his fingers up my thigh. My skin was on fire from that simple touch, but I couldn't tell him. After all, we aren't mates anymore, and we rejected each other.

"It's not like you can do anything anymore. I'm not your mate, and you are not mine. Remember?" I asked.

"You and I both know there are ways for us to get that bond back, but I'll wait," He replied.

"For what?" I scoffed, "Waiting for me is a lost cause and childish dream. Why don't you make some little bastards with one of those bitches in your pack?"

"You never seem to let up on the insults, do you?" He asked, chuckling again.

"No, I don't," I replied, "Now get it through your thick skull that I want nothing to do with you anymore."

"Oh really?" He asked.

"Really," I firmly stated.

"Then why is your thong practically soaked?" He asked.

Chapter Twenty-Three

The sounds of a loud bang outside, followed by growling, caused me to push Jayden away from me. An irritated look had formed on his face at the noisy interruption from outside as he let out a low growl.

"I'll be back so we can continue talking," I assured him. He nodded and sighed loudly before sitting down at the table. I walked outside to find two twin alphas advancing toward Eve, who seemed to be standing her ground, which they didn't like. It didn't take long for me to figure out that these two were the twin alphas that Jayden had told me about.

"What kills me about this situation is that just after we signed this damn treaty, you two decided to harm my friend here," I snarled. They both turned to growl at me while Eve looked over at me worriedly.

"Lani, I have it under control. Don't worry about me," Eve told me. My eyes averted toward me, and I looked at her with a big frown.

"Eve, I'm going to worry about you whether you like it or not because you are my closest friend," I told her. She nodded after a while in understanding, and my attention was back on the two wolves.

"As for you two, don't you think it's a little unfair for you to gang up on a woman like some common street thugs?" I inquired. They both growled like dogs as they glared at me with their yellow eyes. A smirk came upon my features at their boldness.

"Of course you don't; you're men hellbent on getting revenge on me and my loved ones just because I showed your sister what the hell would look like if she kept messing with me," I added. Their eyes followed my every move as I walked around them.

I'm not surprised you two are even doing this anyway. Why? Because it is just like your dogs to hold grudges against everyone in the room except for that one person. That's why the packs filled with people of color don't even fool with you guys, to be honest. You are like those damn school shooters you hear about in the news. You don't kill the one person you have beef with. You kill everyone else who isn't involved," I shot at them. They growled lowly at me.

"Don't ever compare us to those lowly humans," one of the Twins snapped. My attention was now on him as a taunting smile spread on my lips.

"A hit dog will holler," I muttered. He tried lunging for me, but I used my magic to bounce him back. His brother growled at me and tried to do the same, but I flicked my wrist, causing him to crash into a nearby wall. I held him in invisible restraints that were way too powerful for him to escape. His belligerent brother, that had been bounced back, was getting the same treatment.

"Eve, get over here," I murmured. She nodded and walked over behind me.

"And don't think I'm not going to scold you for being pregnant. I'm very disappointed in you for not telling me," I remarked. She looked down at the floor in shame as she walked behind me.

"You'll be scolded for your transgressions," I informed her. Silently, she nodded again and stood behind me. My attention went back to the two alphas who dared to harm me.

"Now, as for you two boys, I think a little punishment will suffice after what you tried to do," I told them, "And I know just the right thing."

"Bitch!" They both yelled.

"Sleep," I softly cooed. They both began to fall unconscious, and I lowered their bodies to the ground and slowly walked toward them.

"What did you do?" Eve inquired.

"Put them in a dream-like state. Once they wake up, they'll never both us again," I grinned like a Cheshire Cat.

"How sadistic of you," She smiled. We both began to laugh together at my actions before the mood turned serious again.

"I'm sending you home immediately," I sternly stated.

"Yes, Amora," She mumbled. I flicked my wrists, and a portal opened to send her home. She stepped through it without another word, and I closed it behind her once she was safely inside. Turning on my heel, I walked back to Jayden was still waiting for me.

When I got back, he talked to his beta James who was holding the capsule with the updated and signed treaty. James noticed me and narrowed his eyes while I gave him a wink. He turned back to Jayden to voice his concerns about my presence while the man in question just laughed it off and assured him that it was alright. James nodded with a grim look on his face and turned to leave. He bumped me on the way out to piss him off, and I used my magic to smack him on his ass.

"Nice ass, James," I smirked. He growled at me and stormed out of the room while Jayden just laughed it off.

"So, did you handle the little problem?" He inquired.

"I did, and your alpha buddies are outside resting peacefully," I responded, "If they continue to be as belligerent and stupid as you told me, then I'll make them and their pack my slaves for all eternity."

"What kind of slaves?" He asked.

"The sexual kind. I've tried doing it with twins before, but half the time, they got uncomfortable and just stopped in the middle. These two seem like the type to be down for it," I explained. He chuckled.

"As usual, you never cease to go beyond the wild expectations others have for you," He remarked.

"Others shouldn't have expectations of me in the first place," I smirked, "They'll only get disappointed in the end."

"Trouble in paradise?" he inquired.

"The only trouble we have in a paradise is my inability to use my legs," I grinned. He rolled his eyes.

"Of course, you would say that," He muttered.

"And when have you ever known me not to say that or anything?" I asked with an amused smile. He thought about it and then nodded.

"You're right," He replied. We both stayed silent for a moment as we leaned against the table together. It wasn't an awkward silence, but a very comfortable one, which was rare between us, to be honest, because we're so used to being in each other's group all the time.

"I'm sorry," Jayden spoke up. My face contorted into an expression of confusion. Why was he apologizing to me? What reason did he have to do this?

"Why?" I inquired.

"Because of how I treated you from the time we met until you rejected me," He answered. It was nice to hear him apologize for that time because it showed that he had some maturity. A small smile formed on my lips.

"Thank you," I replied.

"You're welcome, and don't you have something to say to me?" He asked.

"Like what?" I responded.

"Oh, I don't know; an apology as well?" he teased, and that caused me to roll my eyes at him.

"I don't usually apologize," I replied, "However, for you, I can make an exception."

"An exception?" he cocked an eyebrow. I walked in front of him and put a hand over my heart as I gave a half bow.

"My deepest apologies for my past behavior and my deepest apologies for the childish acts I had committed. I hope that you may forgive me, Amora, for my transgressions so that we may both move this and become great comrades in the future," I recited loud and clear. I stood up straight as Jayden looked at me in shock.

"What was that?" He asked.

"Let's say that if a demon gives you one, they are sincere. The usual apologies you receive from others mean nothing and are just little words to us," I responded.

"So I should count myself lucky with that one, huh?" He smiled.

"Mhm," I nodded.

"Figures," he chuckled, "Let's continue talking about you and your little sperm bank you call a boyfriend."

"Sperm bank?" I laughed. He laughed with me too.

"You know how Fae are. They're just too fertile," he mused.

"Of course they are. It's their punishment for fucking anything that walks," I responded.

"And it didn't work because they still go at it and have more kids than wolves," he chuckled.

"That's true. Thorne has about twelve brothers and sisters on each side," I informed.

"Really?" he asked.

"Mhm. His parents were fucking," I answered.

"Wow. Did they even slow down?" He inquired.

"Hell no. His mom is pregnant again with twins, and they're his dad's," I replied.

"Holy shit. How many kids does his mom have by his dad?" He asked in disbelief.

"At least eight, while the other four are by the chef within their castle," I informed.

"Wow. Fae is a different type of free spirit," He responded.

"Of course, they are," I chuckled, "Always have been, always will be."

He nodded in agreement with a smile.

"What do you say about getting out of here and returning to our old place? The furniture is still there and not gathering dust, especially the bed," He informed me.

"The bed, you say?" I smirked.

"Yeah. I sleep there almost every day to have my own space to myself," He replied.

"Why? I thought you hated that place?" I asked.

"It's not so bad now because I'm practically at peace, and I don't have to worry about anyone barging in every second about minor problems or stupid questions," He answered. I let out a soft chuckle at that statement. When we had to move to the pack house, his pack members always did that, which was a straight-up nuisance for us. There were times when we both wanted to be alone or were forced to be isolated by our parents, and they interrupted many countless times.

It was so aggravating because just about half of them were doing it to annoy the shit out of me. That was something that made me want to kill them all.

"Got tired of someone barging in while you were jacking off?" I smirked.

"That and I couldn't get well-deserved sleep either," He answered. I chuckled.

"Well, that's the price of being an alpha," I told him.

"Yeah, and it sucks," He groaned.

"Remember when you gave me head, and that teenage boy barged into our room? I swear his eyes almost popping out of his head was the funniest thing in the world," I chuckled. Jayden shook his head with a smile.

"I had to threaten the kid not to tell anyone and to forget it," he answered.

"It's hilarious just thinking about the amount of trauma and fear that must have been placed in him after that experience," I giggled.

"Somehow, he thought it was wise to disobey me and open his mouth to others," He frowned.

"Him telling people was the worst thing in the world, and it just showed me that he had no sense of boundaries," I rolled my eyes.

"No, he did not, but let's stop talking about this before I get pissed off," He murmured. We continued talking and joking around as if we were old friends. It was nice to have a moment like this with him instead of one where I would murder him. I wish moments would like this would be a frequent occurrence.

Chapter Twenty-Four

It had been a few days since that treaty signing, and Eve and I were out and about a trendy and vast marketplace within the kingdom. We were here to buy groceries for the house since the fridge was barren due to Eve's pregnancy, and that girl eats more than a horse. If I had known that my best friend being pregnant would be such a pain in the wallet, I would have given this girl a condom and done everything I could to prevent it, although missing out on being an aunt was going to be a bad thing, to be honest.

Speaking of Eve's pregnancy, I scolded her as soon as we returned to my mom's house about her being a mother and what she did. There were a lot of tears on her part, happy and sad, but we understood it because she knew that she couldn't do the things she usually did for her anymore.

"Never in my twenty-one years of living would I think that my best friend would keep something important like this to herself. Especially considering how that entire event could have had some unforeseen, dangerous circumstances that could have harmed you and the baby. I can't believe you kept this from me and still had the nerve to sit here and try to protect me!" I scolded. Eve was currently feeling the full force of my anger at her actions, and she was taking it like an adult.

"Eve, do you realize how stupid that was? Do you realize how irresponsible it was to not only you but your baby? Do you not realize the amount of danger you put yourself and that baby in?" I snapped. She silently nodded.

"A head nod doesn't mean shit, Eve. Use your words," I scolded. She flinched at my tone.

"I'm sorry, Amora," She mumbled.

"You better be, Eve, or so help me; I'll kick your ass after this baby is born," I threatened. Her eyes went down to the floor in shame. As much as I wanted to comfort her and apologize for my harshness, I couldn't. She needs to realize that her actions have consequences, and she needs to realize that what she did was reckless and stupid.

"From now and after the baby is born, you will help me with the coven, which means paperwork only until I say so. I don't need you to physically protect me because I am a big girl, Eve. I can handle myself," I informed her, "I'll find somebody to fill your spot for now temporarily."

"Amora-" She started to say.

"This is what's best, Eve," I responded. A faint salty scent reached my nose, letting me know she was crying. A loud sigh passed through my lips, and I sat beside her and pulled her into my arms for a hug.

"I'm sorry for making you cry, Eve, but you have to realize that I'm only thinking of you and your baby," I murmured, "I can't have my best friend be put in danger when she's pregnant, and that's not fair and would make me a horrible person. You have to see this from my perspective."

"I'm.....I-I'm s-sorry....A-Amora!" She sobbed, "I didn't...I didn't mean to m-make you worry."

"Too late for that," I mumbled. She sobbed even harder at that remark, which I regret even making. I and my smart mouth will get me into trouble one of these days, seriously. Oh, wait. It has.

After our little talk, Eve stopped crying and apologized profusely for her transgressions while I forgave her. I knew she was trying to protect me, but she didn't need to do that anymore since she now had someone else worth guarding, and so did I.

"This place is so crowded," I complained, "Why did you have to eat up all the food?"

"I'm sorry if this baby makes me eat more than I normally do," She responded.

"It's fine or whatever. My little niece or nephew needs all the nourishment they can get," I mumbled, "Even though it is at the expense of my wallet."

"Your wallet never gets any smaller no matter how much you spend, you damn rich kid," Eve remarked.

"I am not rich!" I cried out loud enough for her to hear. She chuckled and continued to inspect the stalls for anything I needed for the house.

"And to think that that damn old hag wants me to fill up her fridge," I hissed lowly. Eve picked up a nice, shiny red apple and sniffed it. She placed it inside the basket floating beside us, and a dozen of those she smelled. It was routine for me to take Eve with me so she could sniff the produce with her heightened sense of smell to tell which was good or bad. When it came to packaged foods, I had to inspect them with my eyes to see if they were good or bad, so we didn't get conned into buying moldy, nasty food.

Times like this make me grateful even to be a supernatural creature because we can all check the food we buy at the market with our heightened senses and other things like illness.

"When is your mom coming back?" Eve inquired.

"Hm? Oh, she's been back since yesterday. She cut the trip short because she didn't want to miss my birthday and because they were getting on her damn nerves," I explained.

"Why did they get on her nerves?" She asked.

"They were acting pretty useless and made her do just about all of the work," I rolled my eyes, "It was pretty annoying."

"I bet," She mumbled. The feeling of a hard yet soft piece of flesh coming in contact with my cheek caused me to fly back into a tree spirit. That same spirit glared at me in annoyance.

"Sorry," I grumbled. The spirit shoved me off them, and I turned to growl at them.

"The fuck is your problem?! I said sorry, you little shit!" I snapped. The spirit became fearful and shrank back.

"I-I'm...I-I'm s-sorry, p-princess," The spirit stammered. A low growl rumbled in my chest as I bared my teeth at the creature.

"Don't let it happen again," I snapped. Standing to my feet, I dusted off myself and searched for the person who hurt me. Whoever it was must have a death wish. Harming me is the worst possible thing you can ever do. My eyes scanned the crowd thoroughly until they finally landed on the smirking face of the biggest bitch in the supernatural community, aside from me.

Lilith.

One of God's angels. My hateful glare turned into that of pure irritation. With a huff, I charged at her like a raging bull and jumped high into the air with my hands clasped together. My hands were brought down hard upon her skull, causing her ground to shake as she was sunk. I managed to make a graceful landing with my powers.

"Amora!" Eve exclaimed, staring at the hole in shock, "You could have killed her!"

"Well, the bitch isn't dead yet, Eve," I snapped, "She's far from it."

"But, Amora-"

"Let's go, Eve. I'm not in the mood to deal with this dumbass," I growled lowly. She nodded and followed after me as we continued our shopping. The hustle and bustle of the market resumed as usual.

"Damn that, Lilith. She's always making cheap shots," I growled under my breath, "I swear one of these days, that bird bitch will get what's coming to her."

Eve snickered at my remark. She was always laughing whenever it came to Lilith and me. She claimed that the only reason why we fight is that "we are such good friends." What a load of shit. I will never be friends with that righteous idiot who takes cheap shots.

"Anyways. When will I get to meet the famous Miguel?" I inquired. Eve's baby's father has always been quite a mystery to me, considering how she has not said a word about him to me. She's kept him a secret from me, her mother, my grandmother, Nyra, and Salem. She refuses to give out any info other than the fact that he is such a great guy. When I asked if she would show a picture, she changed the subject and kept it moving. It's making me a little suspicious of this guy and worried, too, because I don't want him to turn out to be some shady bastard.

"Hmm? Oh well...Uhm....he's off visiting family right now," She lied. How could I tell she was lying? Well, this girl always looks away from me and has this nervous edge to her voice.

"Eve, as much as I love you and respect you, please don't make go into that kind of yours and pull out all the information you have on him," I warned her. She froze in place and looked at me in shock.

"You wouldn't," she gasped.

"I would, Eve. Now set up a meeting between him and me this week, or else," I responded. She sighed loudly.

"Fine. I'll set up a meeting," She mumbled.

"Great. Make sure it's just for him and me. I need to be able to assess him for myself," I replied, patting her head before skipping off to the next stall

"E-Eh!?" She exclaimed. Indeed, she knows how I am by now. If not, she's in for a rude awakening, and so is her baby's father if he doesn't mess up this meeting between us.

A week, and an argument plus silent treatment, later, I was at a café within the human world waiting for Eve's baby daddy to meet with me. Our meeting was set for three, but I decided to go early because this café was my favorite. Since this place was chosen as our meeting spot, hunters were sitting all around me, monitoring me in mundane clothing because I was a "flight risk." Not only that, but Davy had wanted to hang out with me today since it was our day off, and I was fine with it since Thorne was doing his usual duties.

The door to the café opened, and my head raised to see who it was. A tall, handsome guy with straight, jet-black hair pulled into a bun and searched the café for a moment while looking at a photo. His head turned in my direction, and instantly, he smiled. He began walking towards my table. I guess this is the famous baby daddy with Eve acting all types of love drunk and dickmatized.

"Amora?" He inquired with that same friendly smile. Using my powers, I searched his mind for anything that would make me want to kill him and discard his body somewhere unknown. He didn't seem to find it weird that I was doing this, and I guess Eve had warned him. I'm going to hurt that girl when I see her. Doing this type of thing was supposed to be a surprise, a way of intimidation.

Once I was sure that I had found nothing, I stood to my feet with a smile and held out my hand. He took my hand into his and gave it a firm handshake. From what his thoughts and memories told me, he seemed like a genuinely lovely guy with no hidden motives or shady intentions. Hm. Eve did pick a good one this time.

"Nice to meet you, Malakai," I smiled at him. We both sat down across from each other. Now that I look at him up close, he was good-looking beyond my expectations. He had a sharp and prominent jawline, black eyes, russet brown skin, a hooked nose, full lips, and high cheekbones. He had an air of dominance around him that attracted many women to him, even though he had eyes for Eve only, but behind that air was a great man.

"Is it normal for them to be around us like this?" He asked in a low voice. His eyes gestured to the Hunters for a split second.

"Not unless you're a "flight risk" like me," I mumbled. He nodded with understanding while chuckling.

"Eve told me that you can be a dangerous creature when pushed too far," he smirked. "I have to say that I admire that about you."

The sound of his compliment kind of boosted my pride a little. A small smile formed on my face.

"It's nice hearing that from someone outside family and friends. I'm used to having people completely avoid me, so they won't piss me off," I replied.

"Eve has told me some stories about you and your temper, and I have to say that half of them crack me up," he told me.

"Really? Usually, people aren't amused by my antics, especially Eve since she gets dragged into it constantly," I explained, "And just so you know, half the time, she isn't getting dragged into it; she's participating."

He laughed a hearty laugh at that statement. Eve has joined me on my adventures filled with chaos and mischievousness, and she hates to admit that she enjoys them.

"She always tells the story from her perspective about how she hates getting dragged into it," He chortled.

"Well, she's only telling half-truths to make herself look normal," I giggled, "Eve is far from an angel, and coming from me, that's saying something."

"I'll have to take your word for it then," He smiled, "I am a little surprised that she didn't introduce us sooner."

"Me too. From what picking your brain has told me, you are a genuine man, and I know that you'll take care of my best friend in the best way you can," I responded.

"Thank you. I'm so glad that I received your approval," He smiled, "It really means a lot to me, and Eve especially."

"I don't see how. Whether or not you guys date is not my choice to approve. It's up to her," I responded.

"That's true, but she values your opinion as highly as her parent's opinion," he told me. I was a little shocked to hear this, but at the same time, I wasn't because I knew Eve valued my opinion but not to that extent. I'm glad she loves my opinion as highly as her parents' because it shows that I am more like family to her than anything else.

"Honestly, I came here expecting to intimidate you, but there's no need for that since you have shown me how good of a man you are," I started. "However, if you hurt her in any way, shape, or form, I will skin you alive, roast you over a fire like a pig at a Luau, and feed you to your family at your funeral."

He gulped loud enough for me to hear as a smirk spread onto my lips. At least we understand what will happen if he thinks about hurting my friend.

"Now, Eve told me you're meeting my parents today," I changed the subject. He was taken aback by how I casually just changed the subject as if his life wasn't just threatened.

"Uhh...umm....yeah," He replied.

"Well, good luck with that meeting. My dad and mom are very protective of Eve, and so are my grandparents and other relatives, too," I informed him. "My dad, especially, is very intense and graphic about his threats in a way that will make even my mother have nightmares for about a year."

The fear he was giving off at this moment was to be expected, considering how this was a demon king and supreme he was dealing with. He better watches his ass around my dad because he isn't afraid to get his hands extra bloody.

"Just be relieved that you aren't meeting my grandfather. He's much worse than my father, and I combined. He's older, so he's seen very gruesome and ruthless ways of killing and torturing someone, and that's either mentally or physically," I explained, "Despite the threats that may come your way from my father, I'm sure he'll take a liking to you. After all, he considers Eve the second child he never had."

"What about your mom? Is she going to be...umm...intense?" He asked.

"Yeah, she will, but that's our style. We're intense because we hold higher political power than most supernatural creatures. We must have a ruthless and horrifying side that balances out our quiet, just side," I replied. One of the members of the Hunter organization caught my attention with a signal, and I let out a small sigh and nodded at them before turning back to Malakai.

"As much as I would love to continue conversing, I have to get somewhere. It was nice to meet you," I dismissed, outstretching my hand.

"You too, Amora," he shook my hand with a smile.

Chapter Twenty-Five

I pursed my lips thoughtfully. "Why is it that every time we hang out, one of us ends up single in some way, shape, or form?" I asked Davy. He chuckled as he took a sip of his scotch. Davy has invited me to stay with him for a while in the mundane world after somehow finding out that I was given a three-week break from work since my mom had come back. We were in his kitchen drinking and talking for hours on end like we usually do when we get together.

"Because we're bad luck for each other," He answered. There was no way of disputing that when we lost respective partners while hanging out together. Most of the time, it had to do with how much we were hanging together, and for others, it had to deal with the jealousy of our ex. This time it was neither. Why? Because Thorne didn't feel like we were a perfect match for each other and said we should break up. I was a little upset, but oh well, that's life. The only thing I can do is move on with my life.

The most fantastic thing Thorne did was tell me that I could keep the gifts he gave me, such as the expensive designer dresses, the jewels, and many other expensive things that I'm too lazy to list. I'm glad he isn't the type to say, "give me my shot back that I paid for," because that's a real pain, to be honest.

"So, is your mom back to nagging you again?" Davy asked. A loud groan rumbled from my throat.

"Yes, and don't remind me. She's still upset that Jayden and I rejected each other. I can't blame her because my finding my mate is kind of rare, but at the same time, I can still fall in love with someone and have kids with them like any other person. That's one thing they don't mention about us demon slash witch hybrids in the stories," I explained.

"I just thought you had one mate you could only have children with," Davy remarked.

"Yeah, I have one mate and one mate only, but it's not like I'm completely infertile because of that," I responded.

"And did you figure that out?" He asked.

"Hm? Oh well, back in high school, there was this good-looking human who I had fallen in love with. He was everything I was looking for in a man too. After a year of dating, we decided to make love to each other. Fast forward to a month later, I was pregnant, my mom was not happy at all, and neither was my dad," I informed him.

"Wow. What happened to the baby?" He asked curiously. It wasn't a known fact in my world that I had a child when I was a teenager. Only a select few knew, and they were all disappointed in me, and we kept it that way.

"I ended up having the baby," I responded nonchalantly.

"Okay, and where are they now?" He asked.

"The child is currently living with her father," I responded, filling my glass again. He looked at me in disbelief.

"Do you even see the child?" He inquired.

"Uhh, duh. I'm not one to have a child and completely abandon them," I responded.

"Well, if you were, then you wouldn't be the first," He remarked.

"Besides, she only lives with her dad because he wants her to have a normal life," I replied, putting air quotes around normal.

"A normal human life?" He cocked an eyebrow. The reason why my little boy was living with his father is that he's part human. When a demon and a human, or a human and a witch or warlock, have a child, they tend to be late bloomers regarding their powers. It isn't until they hit the age of sixteen that their abilities come into full effect, which is a huge disadvantage for them because they will miss out on a couple of vital years of training that help them to control and use them. It's a sad and cruel fate that half or part-human hybrids must have, but that's life for you.

"Human and demon hybrids, or human and witch hybrids, tend to be late bloomers when it comes to magic and all that stuff, and it leaves them at a huge disadvantage because they must work hard to control their powers," I explained. He nodded in understanding.

"So, pretty much like how some people don't experience puberty until later?" He asked.

"That's one way of putting it," I responded, sipping my drink.

"So, how often do you see him?" He inquired.

"Well, I sneak into his room every night and climb into his bed with him. It wakes him up momentarily, but he cuddles with me until the morning," I smiled softly at the thought of my little boy, "Half the time, I'll stay long enough to send him off to school. If I have free time between paperwork, I go get him from school with his dad."

"Is he used to this routine?" He questioned.

"He is and complains about wanting me to live with them even though he knows how much I have to do with my training or my folks," I answered.

"Do you and his-"

"If you're going to ask if his father and I have a good relationship, the answer is yes. We understand each other and how different our worlds are compared to each other," I replied, "We both understand that we have different obligations that take up our time, but we still manage to be there for our child."

"Hm. That's mature of you," he said. I rolled my eyes at him.

"Shut up," I snapped. He laughed.

"Does he ever stay at your place on weekends and holidays?" he asked.

"Mm... yeah, he does stay with me on the weekends. As for holidays, the three of us stay at my mom's place for Thanksgiving and Christmas, then visit his other grandparents for a little bit," I answered, "However, my son's other grandparents don't like me at all because of what I am."

"Well, maybe if they saw how great of a girl you were, they'd get over their hatred," Davy guessed. A small smile formed on my lips.

"As sweet as those sounds, it's not going to happen. My son's great uncle was killed by a witch three decades ago," I responded.

"Why?" He inquired.

"That same witch I've known since I was a baby was in an abusive relationship with that man, and he almost killed her one day until she finally fought back and killed him instead. For years, his father has had a hatred for witches, and me being half of one is his worst nightmare," I explained, "He needs to get over it, though, because his brother was abusive, and he deserves to die."

Davy chuckled at my statement, then sipped his drink.

"Can't argue with that," He responded, "Anyways, when can I meet this kid of yours?"

"Well, his dad just sent me a message saying he wanted to see me. I guess we can head over now," I murmured.

"Hold on. I gotta get dressed first," he said. With a flick of my wrist, his attire changed as well as mine. He shrugged and downed his drink as I did the same.

"How do we get there? Car or...?" He asked.

"Open the front door, hon. There should be a portal there already," I informed him, "My son and his father live like ten hours away, so I have to take a portal to get to him."

"Ohh," He nodded. We both stood up and walked through the portal together, and the door closed behind us as we began walking.

"Man, I haven't been in these in years. It still amazes me how much witches can do," he looked around.

"Yeah, well, a portal is something I'm used to, considering how I'm always using them," I responded.

"Of course, you're used to it; you're the one who's half-witch," he said. We finally arrived at the door of my son and baby's father's house. My eyes took notice of the cars in front of the house and the driveway, letting me know he had some little gathering. I placed my hand on Davy's shoulder to reach into my boot to get out the house key, which I had a copy of. I unlocked the door for the both of us and soon walked inside.

"Honey, I'm home!" I exclaimed. All eyes were on me as soon as I said that. Most of the eyes of the unknown people landed on Davy and me. Most of the gazes were very judgmental because of our attire compared to theirs. We were a little underdressed, but it's not like I came here for a party or anything like that.

"Mom!" My little boy exclaimed. He walked over and hugged me tightly, and my feet came off the ground due to his sheer strength.

"Oh yeah, this is your kid," Davy remarked with an amused smile.

"You get stronger every time I see you, kid. How have you been?" I inquired.

"I'm doing great, mom. How about you?" He responded.

"Just working, as usual, my beautiful boy. Your grandad and grandmother keep me busy daily with running the coven and torturing humans," I replied.

"You're already doing that to me," Davy muttered. I made a circle in the air, and soon, he was blown back into the door. He grunted from the pain of his back connecting with the door.

"Amora, what are you doing here so early? I wasn't expecting you till next week," Lucas, my son's father, smiled at me. My son put me down, but he continued to cling to me with a smile. No matter how big he gets, he still makes it his mission to follow me around or stick to me like a joey.

"A friend of mine wanted to meet Angel," I informed him. He looked over at Davy, rubbing his shoulder while glaring at me.

"Is this the annoying guy who used to pick on you until your dad scared him?" he asked. Angel and I snickered while Davy just scowled at me even harder. Of course, the father of my son knew about Davy.

"Yeah, this is him," I giggled. Davy snapped out of his, glaring to look at Lucas. The two began to size each other up while flexing a little bit.

"Mom, why are they doing that?" Angel inquired.

"I don't know, sweetie," I responded, "Let's just walk away slowly."

Angel nods and lets go of me as we sneak away from the "alpha" males. We headed towards the kitchen together, which had more dressed-up people.

"What is this party for, sweetie?" I asked my precious little boy, and he immediately rolled his eyes at my question. Whatever was irritating my little boy needed to be handled, and I will not have someone or something upsetting my son when I was not present.

"It's for dad's girlfriend's new job or something like that," He answered. From the tone of his voice, I can tell he doesn't like this woman at all. It seems as if I should meet this woman.

"Angel, what in the world are you doing? Go upstairs to your room now and keep quiet!" A blond woman hissed at my son. My eyebrow raised at the fact that she was talking to my son like that.

"No. I'm staying down here," Angel told her. The woman smiled at her associates around us before trying to grab Angel's arm. That action alone made me stand between her and my little boy.

"And who are you?" She snapped, looking me up and down as if I was dirt on her shoe. This bitch doesn't know who she's speaking to right now, and it shows. Let's hope that when I tell her that, she'll recognize it. If not, I will ensure she does every time she comes near my son.

"I'm his mother," I responded. As soon as she heard that, she nodded and then smugly smiled.

"So, you're the deadbeat I heard so much about," she snarled loud enough for everyone in the kitchen to hear. The whispering and judgmental stares began. All I could do was laugh, which confused people and made some look at me like I was the worst person in the world.

"You laugh when someone calls you a deadbeat? You are truly a horrible woman," she snapped.

"Angel, do you remember that trick I showed you a couple of years ago?" I inquired.

"Uh-huh," Angel answered.

"Good," I smiled lovingly at him, "Turn around and don't look for a second."

He does as I say, turns around, and then begins to sing a son my grandfather used to sing to me when I was little. My attention was back to the pathetic woman before me, and I took my fingers and began to stretch my mouth fully until it began to take up half of my mouth. Sharp fangs began to grow on the side of my mouth, and my tongue started long and pointed like a reptile. The woman looked at me out of horror, as did everyone else. Someone walked into the kitchen, and instantly, I was on them. My mouth stretched open to devour them whole, causing everyone in the room to scream, then run out of there.

My face returned to normal, and Angel turned to look at me.

"Who was that guy you just ate?" Davy asked as he walked in here.

"Hm? Oh, that was just some false human I had conjured up out of mochi. He wasn't real at all, and he was just there to scare people," I explained truthfully. Davy just sighed and shook his head. He should know by now how I am because he's always having to deal with my antics each time we hang out.

"Why did an entire house of people just leave?" Lucas asked, "And five minutes is a record."

"Your girlfriend has been rude to my baby boy, and I had to teach her a lesson," I replied.

"Thank God you got rid of her," He sighed in relief, "She was a major nuisance."

"I bet," I chuckled.

"Anyways, you guys want to watch some movies or something since this stupid party ended?" Lucas asked.

"Sure. If you don't mind us staying over," I answered.

"You're always welcome," Lucas grinned.

Chapter Twenty-Six

I eyed Jayden warily. "....and you know I wouldn't be asking you if I didn't have some level of trust in you," Jayden finished. Silently, I contemplated what he had just asked of me moments ago. I am helping a friend, after all.

"Jayden, you have to realize that this entire proposal is perilous for me, considering how my life is literally on the line," I replied.

"I know. I considered that, and I'm making sure that every precautionary measure is put in place to ensure your safety," he assured. From what he told me, he had thought long and hard about this for a while. Almost two months, to be exact, and he felt he could turn to me of all people about this, even though we ended on bad terms before.

"Are you sure you're doing right by yourself to ask me to do this for you? My behavior when living with you wasn't accepted by you or your, and this whole ordeal will increase it tenfold," I explained.

"I've also considered your behavior too, which isn't a problem for me because I've dealt with it before," he sneered.

"Yes, but the more sinister side of me will be much more dangerous than anything in the world, given the possible scenario. Are you sure you're prepared for this?" I asked.

"I am sure. I've enlisted the help of your mother, Salem, Nyra, and Eve on this matter, as well as your father and Alistair. They have ensured that you have a comfortable and impenetrable living space," He informed me. How thorough of him. It's kind of sexy to hear him talk like this. If only we had stayed mates, then maybe I could have had much more fun with him in the bedroom.

"You've thought this through, and I'm impressed and turned on simultaneously," I smirked.

"Well, of course, I have. Your life is on the line as well as mine," he replied, ignoring the last part of my statement. Man, he's so used to my sexual nature that he's practically missing those parts.

"I have one more thing to ask, though," I told him.

"What is it?" he inquired.

"Will I be able to have an active role in our child's life, or am I just going to be that rich, powerful aunty they have no ties to?" I asked.

"That is entirely up to you, but it would be very much appreciated if you would," he answered. Now that's surprising to me because he would have strong-armed me into being a mother if I had had his children. My, how little Jayden has grown into a respectable man.

"So you're leaving the decision up to me?" I questioned.

"Yes, I am," He nodded.

"How nice of you, but you needn't worry about me not being in the child's life because I love being a mother more than anything," I smiled.

"Somehow, I wouldn't have believed that almost a year ago," He muttered.

"Well, my maturity levels weren't there, and I was acting out then. However, I'm a changed woman now with her whorish tendencies still very much present in her life, but with more responsibilities as a leader," I chuckled.

"Whorish? You're the definition of a whore, and you know it," He remarked.

"And I'm proud to be one," I grinned wolfishly. He rolled his eyes and shook his head.

"Anyways, do we have a deal?" He asked. He stood up from his seat and held out his hand to me, and I let out another chuckle and stood from my seat.

"We have a deal, baby daddy," I shook his hand.

"Good. Now when do you want to do this?" He inquired.

"How about now? I've been pent up for a month because just about every mythological male creature has been avoiding me like the plague," I answered.

"Now....?"He looked confused, ".....in your mom's office?"

Silently, I sauntered over to where he was and pushed him down in the chair. Swiftly, I straddled his lap.

"Ai-"

He was soon silenced by my lips crashing against his in a heated kiss. He resisted at first but began to get into the rhythm quickly. My hips slowly rocked as I ground my crotch against his.

My hands, as if they had a mind of their own, roamed his toned chest before I ripped open the shirt he had on. Buttons flew across the room in different directions.

"That was my favorite shirt," he remarked.

"It'll be fixed later. Don't worry," I assured him.

"You better not forget," he warned.

"Oh, hush. You act like I don't keep my word," I rolled my eyes.

"It's a fifty-fifty kind of thing with you," He responded.

"Hey, hey, hey. Don't forget that this is my uterus you're using," I reminded.

"How can I forget? You're one of the most powerful creatures in the world, and you come sixth in strength," He told me.

"Sixth? Who are the other five?" I asked in confusion.

"Your mom is number one, your dad is number two, Alastair is number three, Nyra is number five, and Salem is number six," He responded.

"Who the hell ranked us like that?" I inquired, feeling slightly irritated.

"Everyone in our world, along with the Hunters too. This is, so every supernatural creature knows who and who not to mess with," He responded.

"Really?" I smirked.

"I shouldn't have told you if you were going to be this cocky about it," He replied.

"Nope," I grinned.

"Anyways, can we continue already?" He asked.

"Eh. I don't know," I shrugged, "I'm one of the most powerful beings and bearing children with someone like you isn't in my best interest."

He narrowed his eyes at me hard as soon as I said that, causing me to giggle.

"Will you just shut up so we can get on with it already?" He asked.

"That tone certainly won't get you anywhere," I teased. He glared even harder at me.

"Amora," He clenched his teeth.

"Fine, fine," I giggled, "We can continue, but let's go somewhere else, like my dreamscape. It's a much cozier place for us to go, plus we can have some privacy."

"I say that's a great idea," Salem spoke up, stalking into the room.

"When did you get back?" I asked.

"Two minutes ago. Damn European bitches get on my nerves," She huffed.

"I'll be happy to listen when I get back, Salem. Just keep watch over things," I commanded.

"Alright. Have fun," she replied. The portal to the dreamscape opened on the floor, and me being the reckless one, I leaned backward on Jayden's lap and pulled him with me.

"What the hell?" He exclaimed. We soon landed on top of an incredibly soft bed with him on top.

"Why do you always do things like this?" He asked.

"Because it's fun," I giggled.

"For who?" He questioned.

"Me," I smiled. He rolled his eyes this time and sat up to look around.

"So this is where you would escape for days on end," he realized.

"Mhm. It's such a nice and cozy place," I smiled.

"It sure seems that way," he noticed, looking around. He moved off the bed and walked around a little.

"Why did you make this an outside world?" He asked.

"It just seemed peaceful this way, ya know," I replied, sliding off the bed.

"I think it's cool," He nodded.

"Thanks," I beamed.

"You ready to do this?" He asked.

"Sure, but I get to be on top," I replied as we walked back to the bed.

"Yeah," He chuckled, "We'll see."

My eyes narrowed at him when he said that.

"I'm kidding, but can you get us some handcuffs?" He asked.

"Why handcuffs?" I questioned.

"They're for me," He answered.

"For you? Ooh. I like this idea," I grinned. Handcuffs dropped from the sky and onto the bed in an instant.

"Where the hell did my handcuffs go?" A familiar voice asked, and the portal closed.

"Who did you steal these from?" He inquired.

"A friend," I answered.

"Oh," he cringed. Without so much as a warning, he had me underneath him. The sound of the handcuffs clicked, indicating that I was the one being handcuffed.

"Oh, you sneaky bastard," I hissed.

"If I let you do it, then I won't be able to fulfill my fantasy," he purred.

"What fantasy?" I asked.

"Having you handcuffed and submissive," he answered.

"Wow. I should've seen this coming," I muttered.

"Mhm. Now, let's get started. We've both got some obligations to fulfill in a couple of hours, and I should fill you with my seed as thoroughly as possible," he husked. Heat pooled between my legs at his words.

"Luckily for you, I'm ready for you to fill me already. I hate when you use protection," I replied.

"Listen here, and I wasn't trying to have kids those other times. Just because you like to be raw-dogged doesn't mean I want to be the one to do it," he mused.

"You're into some rough sex, but you won't consider raw-dogging? Vanilla much?" I shot at him.

"I'll show you who's vanilla," he ripped my top in half.

"Hey! That was my favorite top," I said.

"Whoops," He smirked.

"Bastard," I muttered.

"Do you think it's wise to insult me when you're in this position?" he cocked an eyebrow.

"I don't give a fuck about what position I'm in. You're still a bastard," I responded.

"Well, this bastard is about to make you regret those words," he countered.

Chapter Twenty-Seven

It had been a month since Jayden and I had begun preparing to conceive a child, and let me tell you firsthand that this pregnancy is going by quickly. Because Jayden is a wolf and I'm half demon, our genetics accelerate the pregnancy significantly. I'm technically one month, but I look around three months. In addition to our genes, my half-witch part is weakened, so my magic isn't as strong. It's dangerous to have happened to me because I can't defend myself like I usually do, but luckily, I have Eve by my side to protect me.

"Man, I can't believe the two people who hated each other's guts and wanted nothing more than to kill each other are having a baby," Eve remarked.

"Me neither, but we're past that now. We're both in two different places, and we're both acting like an adult," I responded.

"Hm. Look at you are being all mature," She smiled.

"Shut up. Don't act like you haven't heard me speak like this before," I rolled my eyes.

"I have, but it's a rare occurrence for me, like your apologies. Those are extremely rare and seem like a once-a-month kind of thing," She chuckled. My apology is like a blessing from heaven because it's so rare and unheard of.

"Well, I need to change that anyway. I'm a mom for the second time," I sighed.

"A mom to a part witch, part human, and part demon child and a part demon, part wolf, and part witch child," Eve added.

"I guess I'm mixing the gene pool," I remarked.

"Like kool-aid," She responded. That remark made me laugh because of all the things she could use, and she used kool-aid.

"Well, at least they'll be powerful," I smiled.

"Hm. Davy is probably going to say the same thing as me," She chuckled.

"Oh, you bet I am," Davy smirked, walking into the room with two of his subordinates behind him.

"What brings you here?" I inquired.

"I'm just here to discuss some things with you involving an incident with a witch and to congratulate you on the new edition," he answered.

"For now, I can't handle official matters like that because I'm pregnant, but Salem can," I informed him, gesturing towards the black cat. Davy's subordinates laughed out loud after I said that. It sounded ridiculous that I was telling Davy that Salem would help, but who cares what they think? They're human, after all.

"I don't appreciate you volunteering me for things like this," Salem remarked, jumping onto the desk. A gasp from the two idiots behind Davy made me smirk, and she stretched for a moment before sitting down.

"Hey, Salem," Davy smiled.

"Hello," Salem responded, "How are you?"

"I'm doing fine," Davy replied.

"That's good. Make sure you don't overwork," She murmured.

"I won't, but let's get back on topic. Currently, we have a witch in our custody, a young witch at that," He informed.

"A young witch? How young?" Salem asked.

"Thirteen," He answered.

"What happened?" I questioned.

"She was being bullied by a group of girls at her school, and she accidentally knocked them out," He answered.

"Oh no. Was there a crowd?" Eve asked.

"Yeah. A big one considering how they were in school," Davy sighed. Salem, Eve, and I exchanged worried looks with each other.

"Do her parents know?" I asked.

"Her father knows, but he's an idiot," Davy rolled his eyes.

"What do you mean by an idiot?" Salem queried.

"I mean that he had impregnated her mother thirteen years ago and then somehow gained custody of the child, even though he's extremely prejudiced towards her heritage as a witch," Davy answered.

"What did he do to her?" I asked.

"He beat her so bad that she was hospitalized," Davy answered.

"Did they call CPS?" I inquired.

"Yes. She's going to be taken away from him, but I had to let them know that they weren't dealing with a normal child," He explained.

"And what did they say?" Eve asked.

"They said she's half human, which means she'll stay in the system," Davy answered.

"Over my dead body!" I exclaimed, "They tried that shit on me years ago, and my mom stopped it."

"Is her mother trying to get her back, or are they not letting her? It's alarming that they would even try something like that," Eve worried.

"Her mother is trying, but they're not letting up," He sighed.

"Eve, get ready. We're about to create some chaos," I told her.

"Wait. Wait. Wait," Davy began.

"What?" I asked.

"Make sure you carry this with you when you go. It'll give you some freedom to do whatever you feel is necessary," He answered, handing me a badge.

"Thanks," I grinned.

"No problem," He nodded. The door to the office swung open to reveal a hospital hallway, and we stepped through it together.

"Her room number is 501!" Davy called out to us.

"Thanks," Eve and I spoke.

"Ready?" I asked.

"Definitely," Eve chuckled. We walked towards the girl's room and saw a police officer.

"Whoa, ladies. You can't go in."

"Shut up and move," I flicked my wrist, and the two officers were moved out of the way. We went inside, and a well-dressed older woman was standing there.

"You can't be in here," she warned.

"Oh yes, we can," I held up the badge Davy gave me.

"We already told him that she's going to be in our custody because she's half human," The woman informed.

"Well, this half-human right here is going to get more dangerous as she gets older if she doesn't learn how to control her powers, you ignorant fool," I hissed.

"Let me guess. You're the one he was talking about?" She spoke.

"Yes, I am, and what I say goes. She's coming with me whether you like it or not. She may be half-human, but she's also half-witch, which means that she's going to get more dangerous as she grows," I spat venomously.

"I've heard that in some cases, half-human and half-witch hybrids don't get stronger," she remarked.

"From where? An unreliable human source that doesn't know shit about our world?" I asked, "Half-witch and human children are unpredictable regarding their powers because they are not as unstable as a three-year-old witch but also dangerous. If she continues like this, the next incident won't be just knocking someone unconscious; it'll be death. Do you want to have the blood of innocent children on your hands because you didn't want to listen?"

"We won't know for sure until she-"

"God damn. I'm getting tired of this shit, Amora," Eve snapped, cutting her off.

"Me too," I agreed, looking at the woman menacingly.

"If you ladies so much as take her, the two officers outside will kill you," the woman warned.

"I'll tell you right now that if they so much as try, the father of my children will be here within a millisecond, ready to rip out your throats. Not to mention that my father, the king of demons, and my mother, the supreme of all witches, will come here ready to tear apart every single human within this vicinity, no matter their age," I spat venomously.

"She's right, and the only way you can kill me is if the bullets are pure silver, which I can already tell they aren't," Eve added.

"And I'm simply impossible to kill, but you can try," I smirked devilishly, "Now, quit being a dumb bitch and hand the girl over to our custody before you make a dangerous situation that will get people seriously hurt or killed!"

The room shook with every word I spoke, which seemed to change her mind. If she thinks that I'm some mere witch, then she's mistaken. I'm something she's never seen before and something that she will regret defying for the rest of her life.

"But the courts say that her mother is unfit," She spoke up.

"Whatever judge fucking approved for her to be put in foster care is a dumb ass just like you. Because she's half-witch, she's supposed to be with her mother for the rest of her life. It's within the treaty our leaders created with you humans long ago, or did you just completely skip over it?" I narrowed my eyes at her.

"She skipped it," Eve responded.

"I know she did, and I bet she and her little associates have fucked over many hybrids in the past," I replied.

"Oh, they have, and we're going to see that they suffer for it," Eve grinned devilishly.

"Definitely. Now, she comes with us no matter what, and I don't give a damn about what you say. Her mother will raise her for the rest of her life as best as possible. There's nothing you or that stupid judge can say," I spat. Eve walked from beside me and towards the bed. She picked up the young girl and slung her over her shoulder.

"We'll take our leave now," I announced. With a flash, we were gone.

"That was quick," Davy muttered.

"It didn't feel like it," I murmured, "Also, you need to find out who the judge presided over the custody case. I feel they have been screwing over hybrids and their families for years."

"Already on it. My father has been building a case on him for years, and now an informant of ours got some pretty substantial evidence against him that will take him down for this," He informed.

"Good. As for this little girl, I'm going to heal her wounds and take her to her mother. She'll be delighted to see her," I responded.

"Thank you, Amora," He smiled.

"You're welcome. I'm happy to help a friend and an innocent child in need," I smiled back.

"I don't care about what anyone says. You're the kindest person in the world," He remarked.

"Oh, stop before you make me blush," I beamed. He chuckled and walked over to kiss my cheek.

"That's just a small token of my gratitude," he smiled.

"You are such a charmer," I giggled.

"I know. That's why I'm trying to get into your pants," he smirked.

"You said that out loud?" Eve asked.

"At least he's honest," I shrugged.

"An honest idiot," Eve muttered.

"But he's not getting any from me at all," I announced.

"Damn!" Davy hissed.

"Yeah, yeah. Shut up," I waved him off.

"Can't you at least consider the benefits of giving birth?" He questioned. It is approved by doctors that having sex will make the labor process a little easier. However, I can't have sex with Davy because Jayden will get upset, and he's a possessive idiot.

"No. Sorry," I apologized.

"Damn. Now, I gotta find somebody who sucks my dick as good as you," He muttered.

"My ex's sister is good at that. Well, all of them are," I murmured.

"You mean the prince of Fae?" He cocked an eyebrow.

"Yes. The men in the kingdom talk about her a lot, and all say good things about her. He'll, and she even has a great reputation with the women, even me," I explained.

"You couldn't let me join?" He asked. Quickly, I scribbled Evangeline's, Thorne's sister, number and handed it to him.

"Davy, take her number and leave me alone," I hissed. He laughed, took the paper from me, said his goodbyes, and left.

"You got beaten out by Thorne's sister?" she asked.

"Yeah. It was amazing, and you should talk to her," I responded.

"Maybe one day because my baby daddy is being stupid," She sighed.

"Fae women are some great lovers," I told her.

"I've heard, but the open relationship thing isn't my thing," Eve shook her head.

"There's some Fae who don't partake in that either," I told her.

"Really? Hopefully, I encounter somebody like that," She smiled softly.

"I'm sure you will," I nodded.

Epilogue

After all of that, from pissing off an entire pack, from grappling with my parents on whether or not I can both rule a coven and the demons, and dating on the side as well, I can honestly say that I'm thrilled right now. I've got two wonderful children to look after, a coven to govern, and a kingdom of demons to rule over, and I'm as single as can be.

I'm doing fine all on my own with Eve beside me, and I wouldn't change a damn thing. I will continue doing me for all eternity, and can't nobody stop me; not a man, not a wolf, and not a demon. I will live my life for as long as possible and do what I want. When the fuck I want.

If anybody had a problem with it, they could kiss my ass and go to hell for all I care.

Have I made a lot of people mad with this attitude of mine? Yes. Have I made new enemies? Yes. Will I continue making them? Yes.

Will I continue sleeping around? Yes. Breaking up marriages with different rulers of different kingdoms? Hell fucking yeah, because I don't give a shit.

"Why the hell do you keep breaking up marriages?! Damn slut!" Eve exclaimed, slamming her hand on my desk.

"He was hot. Sue me," I nonchalantly replied.

"You're going to get everybody killed with this mindset," She grumbled.

"Eh. Who cares?" I uttered, clearly bored.

"I do! I'm not about to deal with the angry wives of these rulers!" She snapped, "Not to mention that you had a fucking threesome with the king of giants and his son!"

"Yeah. That was fun," I replied, chuckling.

"Get your act together, or else I'm hurting you!" She snarled. She stormed out of my office, growling under her breath that I would make people go to war over the dumbest things.

"Ugh! Fine," I groaned. Okay. Maybe I can't be sleeping around with different men from different kingdoms because Eve will murder me. It was fun while it lasted.

"God. You're worse than anybody I've ever met," Jayden remarked right across from me.

"Ahh. Who cares?" I shrugged.

"Eve does, and you're going to get murdered by her if you don't quit," Jayden told me.

"I'll quit for her, but that's it," I conceded.

"How does it feel to be a slut?" he inquired.

"Don't know. Ask your mother," I shot at him.

"You know what happens when you talk about my mother like that, right?" he asked.

"How could I forget? Three years ago, you almost broke me," I answered.

"Maybe that would have been a good thing," he joked.

"For who?" I cocked an eyebrow.

"Everybody and their marriages," He responded.

"They were coming onto me. What the hell was I supposed to do?" I inquired.

"Turn them down, stupid," He answered in a "duh" tone.

"Whatever. I'm not turning down good sex," I told him.

"And that's why you're in this predicament now," he rasped.

"Yeah, yeah. Also, tell your buddy Calvin to leave me the fuck alone. He keeps demanding me to come to see him, and every time I do, he fucks up my ability to walk," I said, "He's a sadistic bastard, and I want nothing to do with him."

"You're complaining about somebody being sadistic of all people? Wow. How the tables have turned," he laughed.

"Shut up! Calvin is going to break me one of these days, and it's not going to be funny at all," I hissed.

"Good. Let him," he chuckled.

"God. I'll do it myself," I mumbled.

"Do what yourself?" Davy asked, walking into the office.

"She's going to tell Calvin to back off," Jayden informed.

"Calvin? You'll tell Calvin, the most sadistic alpha in the nation, to back off?" Davy questioned.

"Yes," I nodded. Davy looked at Jayden before the both of them began bursting into laughter. That pissed me off even more. Fucking assholes are laughing at my pain like this is funny.

"DIE! BOTH OF YOU JUST FUCKING DIE!" I yelled. That made them laugh even harder, and I gave them the finger before storming out of my office. I shouldn't be storming out of there when it's my office.

"What happened in there?" Eve asked.

"I told them I'm going to tell Calvin to back off," I answered. She did the same thing that those assholes did, which was laugh. I'm killing all three of them in the most horrific way possible.

"Why is this so fucking funny?!" I snapped.

"Because it is. You know that Calvin isn't going to listen to you," She responded.

"Oh, he lost it," I hissed.

"Whatever. Your dad said adjusting the demon realm to the mortal realm's time has gone successfully. The time difference isn't as drastic as it was before, and it's going to be much better for you to alternate between two different realms," Eve told me.

"Great. I'm glad that it went well," I smiled.

"Me too," She nodded.

"Since that's been settled, I'm going to head to Calvin's place. I need to get this over with already," I announced. She laughed harder once I said that, and I glared at her.

"Fucking asshole!" I hissed, forming a portal, and I stepped through it while she continued laughing her ass off.

After I stepped through, I was outside the entrance of Calvin's large mansion. His guards stood outside looking as stoic as ever, but they opened the gate for me as soon as they saw me. My heart began pounding in my chest with every single step I took.

NO! Don't be nervous, Amora. You've got this. You can do it. Who gives a fuck about Calvin? You're the most powerful witch in the world and can handle him. Yeah. You can do this, Amora.

As soon as I stepped through the door, a smirking Calvin was there to greet me. My eyes took in the sight of him in gray sweatpants, a white t-shirt, and sneakers. He looked so good that I could feel myself starting to-NO! No, Amora, and you will not get distracted by him.

"So you finally decided to come when I called?" He asked.

"I came because I have something to say to you," I responded.

"Oh? What do you have to say?" He inquired, moving towards me. He was now towering over me with that same smirk on his face and his arms crossed.

"I came to tell you to chill out when we have sex. You're a great partner and all, but I don't like it when it's hard for me to walk," I responded.

"Okay," he chuckled.

"Okay? That's all?" I questioned.

"Yes," he nodded, "I'll try not to do it so hard."

"Really? Thank you," I smiled.

"You're welcome, but don't think that because I've agreed to be lenient on you that you don't deserve a punishment for not answering me," he told me.

"Huh?" I questioned, feeling my heart drop.

"I'm going to make you regret not answering me," He responded. He hoisted me over his shoulder with ease. He carried me up the stairs and smacked my ass hard. A loud yelp escaped my lips.

"You're not gonna leave my home for another three days," he warned.

"Three days?! Oh no," I tried to get him to set me down, but he held onto me.

"Don't struggle, Amora. You're not going to change my mind at all, and you know how long I can go," he smirked, chuckling darkly. Somebody save me now, and a literal demon will torture me. Please help me before he leaves me a broken mess.

I'm glad he agreed to go a little easier on me, but he's not going easy on me simultaneously. He's going to make me suffer as much as he can, and he's going to enjoy every single second of it.

This will make those three idiots laugh even harder when they hear about this, but I'm not giving them the benefit of that.

True to his word, he didn't go easy on me at all. My legs felt like jelly, and he was cuddling me in his bed with a smug expression.

"I've let Eve know that you won't be back for a couple of days," he smirked. The only response he received from me was silence. Fucking asshole.

"If there's one thing I want to say to you, it's that I want you to marry me," He said.

"Marry you? What the hell?" I exclaimed, moving away to look at him. He expected me to marry him when I spent most of my time avoiding him. He must be crazy.

"Marry me," He repeated.

"What? Why?" I asked.

"Because I like having you beside me and in my bed," He told me.

"No. I'm not about to be discarded when you find a mate," I shook my head.

"I've already had a mate before," he informed.

"And what happened to her?" I inquired.

"She was too weak for me. She cried too much and was always trying to change me," He responded, "Unlike her, you don't try to change me."

"Because there's no changing you. You're a stubborn man, and you do what you want," I snapped.

"And you're the same way, my sweet," he replied, "So what do you say?"

"Can I sleep with anybody I want to?" I inquired.

"No," he replied darkly.

"Then no," I shook my head.

"Why would you want to sleep with anybody else when I can satisfy you more than they can?" he asked.

"Because I like the idea of having the freedom to sleep around with no strings attached," I answered.

"You'll only marry me if I let you?" he questioned.

"Yes," I nodded.

"It's either you marry me, or I'll make sure that every last one of your boy toys is sent a video of you on your knees telling them that you're taken," he told me.

"What the fuck, Calvin?! You wouldn't dare," I hissed.

"Try me," he stated. My eyes searched his for any indication that he was bluffing. When I saw that he wasn't, I cursed under my breath.

Fine," I growled, "I'll marry you."

"Glad you see it my way," He smirked, leaning back against the headboard. He's a bastard that does what he wants, but now he's a bastard I will be married to for all eternity. Fucking asshole.

"And don't worry, I won't be such a bad husband. I'll treat you better than any other man you've been with. I'll even make sure that your children are treated as my own," he assured me.

"You were going to do that whether you liked it or not," I hissed.

"Yes, I know, mama bear," he smiled, chuckling.

"You're the second man in my life who resorts to such underhanded tactics," I muttered. My father was at the number spot for underhanded tactics, and it's how he finally got my mother to become his wife.

"Hmm...I'm glad," he responded.

"Ugh. My freedom. My sweet precious freedom," I sighed.

"On the bright side, I've finally obtained the most unobtainable woman," he remarked.

"So I'm a prize to be won?" I snapped.

"A little," He answered jokingly.

"Oh fuck off," I snarled. He chuckled with a smile.

"Thank you," he grinned.

Ugh. This bastard has now thwarted my plans of being single for the rest of my life. He's such a vindictive piece of shit, and I hope he kicks the bucket before I do.

Ugh. I'm stuck to this bastard for the rest of my life and can't do a thing about it. Killing him will only start a war, and I can't think of anything else.

This epilogue has turned into a real shit show, and I'm ready to kill the author for even doing this to me. She's such a bitch for doing this to me. She could have let me live happily ever after, but she fucking didn't, and now I'm being punished for the rest of my life.

ABOUT THE AUTHOR

Jade Lafontaine is a pen name for a bestselling paranormal romance author best known for her werewolf fated mates romance novels. This is her first fantasy novel that isn't a romance. In her free time, Jade enjoys gaming, gardening, and doing arts and crafts with her family.

www.ingramcontent.com/pod-product-compliance
Lightning Source LLC
LaVergne TN
LVHW050534160826
845677LV00011B/2030

* 9 7 9 8 3 6 0 2 4 1 2 1 8 *